His mouth twitched, bringing the dimples to his cheeks. "Don't mail any more old letters before asking the sender's intention."

Leah nodded. "You can bet on that. I hate to think what Mom's going to say when she sees me. I know she's terribly embarrassed."

His head dipped to one side and the cornflower-blue eyes rested on her. "What kind of surprise did you plan?"

"A bit of organization. That's what I do. I help people eliminate the excess accumulation that's weighing down their lives."

Leah removed a business card from her pocket and handed it to him.

He studied it briefly, nodded and shoved it into his coat pocket. "I have to go."

"Again, I'm really sorry.

His gaze lingered on her face. "It was unintentional. And I'm embarrassed by my behavior. Just forget I came by. Forget you ever heard the name Josiah Byrd."

At the door he paused and pressed the doorbell again, a smile crossing his face. "I thought that was the Carolina fight song."

Leah pumped her arm in a

"Go Heels."

He chuckled and kept walk

Forgetting was easier said th

TERRY FOWLER

is a North Carolina Tarheel by birth and choice. She's lived in North Carolina for her entire life and can't think of any other place she'd rather be.

Reading has always been a love of hers and she once wanted to be a librarian. Little did she know that books would play a different role in her life.

By day she works as administrative support staff for the local water and sewer authority, but by night she becomes Terry Fowler, Author. She doesn't wear a cape or anything glamorous like that, but she does hang out with some interesting characters.

She fully believes that following God's plan for her life is the reason for her success and prays that every story she creates gives God the glory.

Her other interests include working in her church, reading, gardening and spending as much time as possible with her family.

TERRY FOWLER

Unintentionally Yours

HEARTSONG
PRESENTS

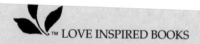

Recycling programs for this product may not exist in your area.

™ LOVE INSPIRED BOOKS

ISBN-13: 978-0-373-48662-5

UNINTENTIONALLY YOURS

www.LoveInspiredBooks.com

Printed in U.S.A.

Forget the former things; do not dwell on the past.
—*Isaiah* 43:18

This book is dedicated to the perfect father—
Our Heavenly Father. The one who loves us
despite our failings and who will always be there
if we accept Him.

As always, thanks to Tammy and Mary for your help
in producing this book. You give such wonderful
feedback, it would be difficult to do this without you.

Chapter 1

"Come on, Champ." Leah Wright tugged gently on the leash in hopes of motivating the elderly dog. "Please, Champ. Just a short walk and then you can have your afternoon nap."

She frowned when the Welsh corgi stretched out on the cool tile of her parents' kitchen floor, lifting his head now and again to nibble at the food in his bowl.

"Honestly, you have to be the laziest dog that ever roamed the face of this earth. Or maybe you're a miniature donkey. You're stubborn enough, that's for sure."

Her grumbling didn't affect him in the least. Leah didn't have time for this. She wanted to get on with her plans, not wait around all day for Champ to decide he was ready for exercise.

The University of North Carolina fight song filled the house. The doorbell. Her parents loved the gift from a college pal. Leah found it a bit strange but supposed it was their way of showing support for their alma mater.

She wondered who could be at the door at this time of day. Probably a family friend who wasn't aware her parents were away. She dropped the leash and told the dog, "I'll be back."

Champ rose and ambled after her, the leash trailing behind him. He barked with the song.

Now he moves, Leah thought. "Hush," she told him, not surprised when he continued to bark.

The bell rang again. Surely her parents' friends wouldn't ring the doorbell incessantly. "I'm coming." Leah hurried through the dining room and into the entry hall. She gingerly pushed the curtain aside and peered outside.

A stranger. Handsome with his sweet face and dimples, but he looked angry. Leah hesitated, not sure what she should do. *Don't be silly,* she told herself. Something could have happened or maybe he had the wrong house. She unlocked the dead bolt and pulled the door open.

"May I help you?" she asked. Champ continued to bark and she stepped on his leash to stop him from running outside.

The man waved a flowery envelope in her face. "Are you Marty Washington? Uh…" he lifted the envelope and read the label "…Martha Wright?"

Leah recognized the envelope as one she'd mailed earlier in the week. With her parents out of town, she'd decided to surprise them by doing the organization she'd been trying to talk her mom into for months. The letter had been sticking out from underneath the blotter on her mother's desk, so of course she'd mailed it.

"She's my mother. She goes by Marty. I'm Leah."

"Josiah Byrd."

He handed her a card. Leah glanced down and saw from the photo that he was the Byrd in Byrd Realty, a well-known local commercial real estate company.

"Your mother wrote this letter nearly thirty years ago." He slung the words in accusation. "Dad's deceased. I'm curious as to why anyone would mail such garbage after so long. She was obviously angry, and the allegations would break my mother's heart."

Dread and surprise swamped Leah. What had she done? What did the letter say? Fighting back her urge to blame the lateness of delivery on the post office, to say it was a miracle it showed up after all this time, she frowned and said, "I'm sure you're wrong. My mother would never intentionally hurt anyone."

"Well, according to what she wrote here, she was gunning for my dad."

Offended, Leah said, "That isn't something my mother would do."

"Read this." He thrust the letter at her.

Leah pushed the envelope away. While she might be curious about the contents she had no intention of reading anyone's personal communication without their permission. "It's none of my business. Why would you read a letter that wasn't addressed to you?"

Not bothering to hide his disgust, he said, "Because someone mailed it and Dad's not around to read it." Josiah crumpled the envelope in his large extended fist. "And if it's true, my father kept major secrets from my mother."

Leah wished he'd stop flapping that letter around. And explain what he was talking about. Was he saying her mother was a liar? "I'm sure Mom can explain."

"She had no business writing him in the first place. He was a married man."

Anger didn't suit Josiah Byrd. His youthful face showed a gentility that had little to do with anger. "My mother is happily married to my father. They recently celebrated their thirtieth anniversary and are on their second honeymoon. I still say you had no business reading her letter. Isn't that against the law or something?"

Suddenly he looked taller and loomed even larger as he stood there in her parents' doorway frowning down at her. His blue gaze narrowed with disdain. "Look, lady, I'm not here to argue legalities with you. Just tell Marty Washington or Martha Wright or whatever she calls herself that my father is dead and there's no reason for any more of these letters."

Leah struggled to project the same image, pulling herself up to her full five-five height. "I mailed the letter and I'm sure my mom can explain why she wrote your father. Come in. We'll call her right now."

When Champ refused to move, Leah bent to lift the unwilling dog and carried him back inside. Josiah Byrd followed them into the entry hall. She unsnapped the leash and set Champ on the floor. When he darted for the door, Josiah blocked him and pushed it closed.

Leah lifted the cordless phone from the end table and hit the redial button. She'd talked with her mother an hour before. They were visiting her Aunt Gwen in New York before leaving for Spain.

"Hey, Aunt Gwennie. May I speak to Mom?"

"Sure, sweetie. Hang on."

Marty Wright came on the phone. "Leah? Is something wrong?"

"There's a guy here. His name is Josiah Byrd." Her mother's gasp disconcerted Leah. "He has the letter you wrote his dad. I told him you could explain."

"How did he get that letter?"

Her mother's cold, accusatory tone made Leah nervous. She didn't much want to admit her role in the situation. "I mailed it for you."

A distinct pause crossed the miles. "Oh, Leah, what have you done? I never intended for that letter to be mailed."

"But why else would you write it? It was addressed and sealed."

"I needed closure for something that happened a long time ago."

Leah grimaced, squeezing her eyes shut. She'd really done it this time. "I see."

"I doubt that." There was no hint of forgiveness in her mother's tone. "I suppose he's furious?"

Leah opened her eyes and studied Josiah's expression. He had a lot going for him with that cleft in his chin, smooth shaved face and thick dark hair. "Yes. He said the allegations could have caused his mother grief."

"No allegations. All truths. Put him on the phone."

Leah handed over the cordless and eavesdropped on their one-sided conversation. Her skin warmed as she considered Marty Wright's embarrassment. Leah knew she should have asked. But in her defense, it looked like a letter that had been forgotten.

"I see," Josiah said a couple of minutes later. "As I told your daughter, I need to be certain this doesn't happen again. Today is the one-year anniversary of my father's death. It hasn't been a good year for my mom." He paused and Leah knew her mother was expressing sympathy for his loss. "Thank you. Sorry to have bothered you."

He turned the phone off and handed it back to her. "I apologize for my outburst."

"I'm so sorry," Leah said. "My parents are away and I thought this was the perfect opportunity to surprise Mom."

He flashed a wry smile. "And instead you got surprised?"

Leah grimaced. "And you. I'm so sorry that I upset you today of all days." She paused, at a total loss as to how to make amends for the situation. "I feel really bad. Is there anything I can do?"

His mouth twitched, bringing the dimples to his cheeks. "Don't mail any more old letters before asking the sender's intention."

She nodded agreement. "You can bet on that. I hate to think what Mom's going to say when she sees me. I know she's terribly embarrassed."

His head dipped to one side and the cornflower-blue eyes rested on her. "What kind of surprise did you plan?"

"A bit of organization. That's what I do. I help people eliminate the excess accumulation that's weighing down their lives."

Leah removed a business card from her pocket. She'd taken them with her earlier when she went to the store, pinning a few on the service board.

He studied it briefly, nodded and shoved it into his coat pocket. "I have to go. Mom's waiting for me."

"I'm really sorry."

His gaze lingered on her face. "It was unintentional. And I'm embarrassed by my behavior. Just forget I came by. Forget you ever heard the name Josiah Byrd."

At the door, he paused and pressed the doorbell again, a smile crossing his face. "I thought that was the Carolina fight song."

Leah pumped her arm in a weak imitation of a cheer. "Go, Heels."

He chuckled and kept walking.

Forgetting was easier said than done, Leah thought as she watched him run down the sidewalk to his big navy blue truck parked in the street.

The phone rang and Leah glanced at the caller ID. Just as she thought. Her mother.

"Has he left?"

Leah glanced up to see the flash of taillights as his truck stopped at the end of the street.

"Yes. I'm sorry, Mom. I had no idea."

"Please tell me you're not reorganizing my house."

Leah knew she'd better come clean. "Just a little. I wanted to surprise you."

"Well, stop whatever it is you're doing. You've already surprised me enough."

She recalled her mother's stern tone from past chastisements. "I came over to feed the animals and thought I'd take care of a few things while I was here. You did tell me to mail those payments."

Her mother had never fully subscribed to the idea of a clutter-free home. She thought it was fine for those who chose to live that way but said it wasn't for her.

"You have no idea what's important to me, Leah. And while I understand your philosophy toward clutter, it doesn't mean I support you going through my home and making decisions that affect me and your father when we're not there. You need to stick with your clients. The people who choose to have you toss their belongings."

"Yes, ma'am. Is it okay if I clean my old room?"

"No. I cleared that room after you moved out. There's nothing in there but items I want to keep and things I thought you might want one day for your kids."

She gave up. "Okay, Mom. I'll stop."

"Thank you."

"Will you explain about the letter?"

Marty Wright sighed heavily. "I once thought Joseph Byrd would play a part in my future."

That shocked Leah. "Does Daddy know?"

"He does. The relationship with Joseph was over before we started dating."

"What happened?"

"He married someone else."

"Josiah's mother?"

"Leah." Her groan sounded so close Leah could almost feel her mother's breath. "I don't want to talk about this. It's in the past and needs to stay there. Your father is the perfect man for me. I'm thankful God intervened in my relationship with Joseph."

Utter misery filled her. "Oh, Mom, I can't tell you how sorry I am to remind you of this, particularly now."

"It's okay, honey. You didn't know."

Leah refused to be comforted. She had caused someone she loved and a complete stranger pain. "I feel bad about Josiah, too. His dad's dead. I wonder what happened to him. He couldn't have been that old."

"Joseph was the same age as your father and me. It was cancer. I read his obituary in the paper."

Leah sighed at the sad news.

"Don't beat yourself up. These things happen in life. We have to roll with the punches."

"But I hate being responsible for the pain of others."

"Then it's a lesson well learned. Don't take it upon yourself to handle other people's business."

How many times had her mom told her to mind her own business? Would she ever learn? "Yes, ma'am. Prayers for a safe flight."

Her parents were scheduled to leave for Spain around 7:00 p.m. Ben Wright had shocked his wife when he presented her with the itinerary the night of their anniversary party. She'd always wanted to travel and he'd said neither of them was getting any younger and they should visit the places they'd talked about over the years.

Leah had cried nearly as much as her mom. She hadn't realized her father could be so romantic. She longed to find the man God intended for her and have the same kind of relationship but thus far her Mr. Right had stayed away.

"Okay, Mom. Give Daddy my love and have fun."

"We will. And Leah, no more reorganizing. Understood?"

"Yes, ma'am. No more reorganizing."

Chapter 2

Josiah settled in his pickup truck and glanced back at Leah Wright standing in the open doorway talking on the phone. Her brown hair was drawn back from her face in a ponytail that hung down her back. Her solemn expression and huge chocolate brown eyes had changed with lightning speed when he'd angered her with his accusations directed at her mother. They'd become sad when she'd come to understand her own role in the situation.

Maybe he should hire her to remove his excess accumulation. He certainly carried a full load of mental baggage.

What had he been thinking to come here, and on a holiday? He'd taken Friday off and used the long weekend to attend a college friend's wedding. He'd returned home that morning and stopped by the office. He'd found the letter in the stack of mail on his desk with a Post-It note from his assistant. She'd wanted to know if she should forward the letter to his mother. It still gave him chills to think what would have happened if she'd done that without asking.

The Wrights lived in one of the more prominent older neighborhoods of Wilmington. His mother lived a few miles away in one of the newer gated communities.

Josiah drove to his mother's home and parked, taking time to remove the letter from his pocket and hide it in the glove compartment. He needed to destroy that thing. The sooner, the better. He supposed he should have returned it to Marty Wright but he couldn't. He had to be sure the letter never surfaced again. Never found its way into his mother's hands.

Marty Wright said she'd written the letter as closure. She'd made references to the pain and embarrassment his father had caused her. She'd even gone so far as to say she hoped never to see him again and prayed God would protect his wife and child. The ranting of a scorned woman? Somehow Josiah didn't think so. He had read the pain in between the lines. Even seen what he thought were dried tears. His father had hurt this woman.

Josiah thought of the bundle of photos he'd found in his father's desk when he moved into the office. A much younger Joseph Byrd in his football uniform with his arm slung about the shoulders of various young women. There was one young woman and another uniformed man who appeared in more photos than the others. He'd started to toss them but hadn't, thinking they were part of the puzzle that made up his dad.

He considered his mother might want to see them one day but wondered why his father kept them at the office instead of at home. Maybe he hadn't wanted his wife to know about these women in his past. What had happened between Marty Wright and his father? He wanted to know but Joseph Byrd had taken that truth with him to the grave.

He found it surprising his father's old flame lived here in Wilmington. Based on what he'd read, Josiah assumed they'd met in college. Had Marty Wright attended high school with his parents?

His mother came out of the house and Josiah jumped out of the truck to help her. She carried an armful of colorful spring flowers he knew she'd cut from her garden. Josiah locked the front door and escorted Cecily Byrd to the car she'd left in the driveway. She didn't care for his vehicle, refusing to climb up into the truck when she had a perfectly good car to drive.

Josiah bent to kiss her cheek. She lifted the flowers. "I think Joseph would have enjoyed these, don't you?"

"He would. He loved that garden, too."

His mother's plants flourished with the love she showered on them. She'd completed the Master Gardener course at the Arboretum and volunteered when her schedule allowed. She had worked wonders with the yard. She'd known exactly what she wanted and gone about getting it done.

"Ready?"

She nodded and Josiah opened the passenger door and helped her inside. They chatted as he drove over to the large cemetery near Shipyard Boulevard. He parked next to his father's grave and waited while she knelt and touched the photo mounted in the flat marker with such longing he couldn't bear to watch.

Josiah busied himself opening the gallon of water he'd brought along and filling the vase in hopes of giving the flowers a fighting chance of survival for more than a day or so. Cecily artfully arranged them. He screwed the lid back on the jug and glanced down to find tears in his mom's eyes. Josiah helped her to her feet and pulled her into a hug. They stood there in silence until she spoke. "I miss him."

"I do too, Mom."

Josiah did miss his dad. While their relationship hadn't been great and his emotions were mixed, he missed having his father in his life. He had always hoped that one day they would settle into a comfortable relationship and put the anger and rebellion of his teen years behind them. He'd never wanted to hurt his dad; he just wanted his love.

Josiah had looked forward to falling in love and producing a couple of children but it hadn't happened. Now his life had stalled. Since his father's death, nothing seemed to be going right. Wasn't today proof of that? Who else could intercept a letter from his father's old girlfriend and make an idiot of himself in front of her daughter?

He hugged his mother a moment longer and stepped back. "Let's go home."

She took his arm. "I made all your father's favorites. I thought a good meal would be the best way to honor his memory."

Josiah smiled. Cecily Byrd believed food cured all ills. "I agree. A good meal is exactly what we need." He guided her toward the car.

Back at the house, Josiah loosened his tie and pulled it over his head. He shoved it in his coat pocket and laid the coat over the chair back. Too bad he didn't have something cooler and more comfortable to wear. Suits and dress shirts weren't the best summer attire.

"What's this?" Cecily bent to pick up something.

He recognized the business card Leah Wright had handed him earlier and reached for it. "Must have fallen from my pocket."

She read the text and looked at him curiously. "Clutter-free? A clutter consultant? What on earth?"

"I met this woman today who comes in and helps clear the junk away. Sounded like a good idea."

His mom looked at him with increased interest. "Actually, it is. I was thinking just this week that I need to do something about your father's things."

The timing was all wrong. She didn't need this. Not today. "Mom, you don't have to…"

She patted his cheek. "Yes, Josiah, I do. It's been a year. You've handled the business, the will and other important matters but there's more to do. I just don't know where to start. It's overwhelming."

"Maybe we can find someone to help."

Cecily held up the card. "What's wrong with this person? Why can't I bring her in to assist me?"

Warning bells clanged in Josiah's head. No way. His mother couldn't work with Leah Wright. "We don't know anything about her."

"Would we know anything about anyone we hired? It's a very cute card." Before he could answer, she asked, "If you don't know her, why do you have this?"

Her hopeful expression forced his response. "We didn't go on a date, Mom. Just exchanged business cards."

"Is she a nice woman?"

"I suppose." There had been something about Leah. Not an in-your-face kind of beauty but she struck him as the kind of person who would interest him if it weren't for the situation.

"You could do with a nice woman in your life. You're not getting any younger and I want grandchildren. All my friends say how lovely it is and I don't want to miss out."

"I date." Josiah felt mulish. Every time he saw his mother she started on her favorite subjects. Him, in love and married, with a house filled with grandchildren. Did she think he wasn't trying?

"I want nothing more in life than to see you happily married with children. You'll be a wonderful husband and father."

Josiah wasn't so sure of that. His dad hadn't been much of a role model. Oh, no doubt Joseph Byrd had unplumbed depths in other areas. How many women had there been in his life? He knew of one and based on what she'd written, there had to be many more.

Cecily squeezed his hand. "Don't look so troubled. You'll

do things your way. And when the time is right God will provide the right wife for you." She held up the card. "May I keep this? I might give this woman a call." She shook her head in wonder. "A clutter consultant. In my day, we never considered the need for such work."

In the past, people held on to things out of necessity. There hadn't been an overabundance of possessions. "Things have changed, Mom."

"Exactly what I want to discuss with you. I need a change. I want to lease a condo at the beach."

Chills ran up Josiah's spine. What had gotten into his mother? "But Mom, you love this place."

"I do, but it's more house than I need now that your father's gone."

He looked down at her. "Where will those grandkids hang out if you move to a smaller place?"

She flashed him a mocking smile. "We'll cross that bridge when we come to it. I don't need five thousand square feet to live by myself."

What had set his mom off tonight? Things hadn't changed in a year. Why now? "You need to sleep on this idea."

Her gaze fixed on him. "I have. For months I've awakened to creaks that made me think someone was in the house only to find it was my imagination. I don't like living alone, even knowing there's an alarm system."

Josiah had a sudden visual of her checking under every bed and in every closet before going to bed. Why hadn't he thought of that? His mother had never spent a night by herself until his father died. "Why didn't you tell me?"

The stubborn determination he knew so well gushed out when Cecily spoke. "Because I refuse to burden you with my fears. Besides, I always loved the beach and your father hated it. Whenever I suggested a beach vacation, he told me to go alone. Every vacation was always some historic battleground."

Josiah recalled many trips centered on historic sites. He'd wondered why they couldn't visit an amusement park like his friends. "I suppose buying this house was his accession to your love of water?"

"Probably. Most summers my girlfriends and I lived at the beach. A couple of families had cottages and they invited me along as company for their daughters. I had the best time."

Her rapt expression held his attention. Josiah could see she really wanted this.

"I long to walk along the beach and enjoy the sunshine. To feel the sand under my feet and the waves against my body."

Josiah held up his hand. "Okay, we'll call Renee. She'll know what's available."

"I already know where I want to go."

His brows rose. She must have given the matter a great deal of thought.

"Richard and Sally have a rental unit at Topsail Beach that would suit me perfectly. A two-bedroom condo. I might even live there full time."

"A condo? What about this house?"

She shrugged. "You could always rent your place and move back here."

Josiah couldn't see himself rambling about this big place alone, either. But he didn't want to see his parents' dream house go up for sale. His mom had reasons for not wanting to be here now but that could change. He'd never lived there but remembered the time and effort she had put into every decision when building her home. He didn't want her having regrets after she'd given it up. "I'd have to think about it."

"Do. I'll show you the brochure Sally gave me after dinner. I'm thinking I'll sign a six-month lease, possibly with an option to buy. Even if I don't live there, beach property is always a good investment."

Whoa. Things were moving too fast. "I'm not kidding, Mom. You need to think about this."

"I have. Every night that I've been here alone hoping you'd stop by for a visit or some of my friends would call and ask me to join them. Evidently there's a rule about widows not being invited to join her married friends' outings."

He trailed her into the kitchen where she set about preparing to serve the food. She handed him a bowl of green beans. "Put that on the sideboard, please. And be careful. It's hot."

Josiah did as requested and returned to the kitchen to carry the slow cooker into the dining room. They served their plates with roast, mashed potatoes and green beans. He drew out Cecily's chair before going around to his own chair.

He took a yeast roll from the basket and passed it to his mom. "Did you indicate you'd like to go out with them?"

Cecily returned the basket to the table without taking a roll. "I've hinted but they're either not interested in having me around or are particularly dense. Maybe they consider me a threat because I'm single. My goodness, that sounds silly, doesn't it?"

TMI, Josiah thought. His parents' romantic relationship had never been something he cared to explore. And definitely not his now-single mother's plans for the future. And he was sure her friends didn't mean anything by their lack of invitations.

"Mom, I'm sorry I've been a bad son. I work long hours and then go home and crash. It's all I can do to get to church and the gym and maintain relationships with my friends, or date in hopes of finding the future mother of your grandchildren."

"That's what I'm trying to say. You have your life. I need one of my own."

"If I'd known you were feeling this way I could have arranged a night out."

Her offended expression spoke volumes. "I don't want you spending time with me out of pity, Josiah. I had an active social life before I met your father and we had one while we were married. I plan to enjoy my golden years. Now say grace and let's eat our dinner before it gets cold. And then I want to hear about your week."

That night left Josiah shaken to his very core. First that letter and now this sudden change in his mom. Sure, he hadn't spent a lot of time with her lately but life had been busy. Most nights by the time he remembered to give her a call it was too late. He'd plan to do it the next day only to become preoccupied with something else until it was again too late to call. He needed to do better.

He understood her need for change. Hadn't he wanted the same for himself all these years? Change in his relationship with his father? His career? His life?

Downtown, Leah struggled with her feelings of remorse. How could she have done this to her mother? No doubt she'd been humiliated by Josiah Byrd's accusation. And she couldn't remember the last time her mother had used that tone with her. This one must rate pretty high on the my-kid-messed-up scale.

She should have known better. How many times had she offered to organize her parents' house only to be turned down? She'd only wanted to help but her mom had put a stop to that. Leah needed to do what they had requested, keep an eye on the house and take care of their pets. Period.

Not that Champ and Lady needed much attention. She often arrived to find the Welsh corgi sleeping on his bed in the sunlight, the Siamese cat curled up on her parents' bed or underneath depending on her mood. Leah often wondered if they had moved since her previous visit. Both animals were getting on in years. Still, while she was there, they trailed along behind her. Leah knew they missed her parents.

The whole thing had started simply enough. She'd brought in the mail, sorted and tossed the junk mail and stamped the bills that needed paying. She'd spotted the edge of the letter peeking out from underneath the blotter just before she went to put the outgoing mail in the box. Thinking her mom had forgotten, she'd added an address label and stamp. Look at the trouble she'd caused.

Chapter 3

Leah jerked and dropped the suspense book she'd been reading when the tune played loudly on her cell phone. She really needed to change that ring tone. It was obnoxious.

"Hi. Is this Leah Wright?"

She fumbled around for the book and put a bookmark in place. "Yes, it is."

"My name is Cecily Byrd. My son had your business card and I wanted to discuss the possibility of your doing some work for me."

Cecily Byrd? Her son? Suddenly it dawned on Leah that she must mean Josiah. Surely he hadn't given his mother her card. Not after their encounter. It had been three days and she'd thought him gone forever. She'd pretty much followed his suggestion and forgotten his existence except for the occasional twinges of remorse.

Still the prospect of doing organizational work prompted her next question. "What did you have in mind, Mrs. Byrd?"

"Well, I'm not sure exactly what you do as a clutter consultant but I need help getting my home organized. If you can't do it, perhaps you can recommend someone else."

Wariness filled Leah. Should she do this? Would her presence upset Josiah Byrd further? But what choice did she have? At times, self-support took precedence over everything else. "I'd love to talk with you."

"Wonderful."

Myriad questions floated through Leah's head but she opted to save them for later. "Is there a time you'd prefer? I can come to your home if that's easier for you."

"Are you available this afternoon? Say around two."

Leah wished she could say it wasn't a good time but her specialty work had taken a hit with the economy. People spent their money on necessities and did the best they could with their organizational efforts. Plastic storage bins were cheaper than human organizers.

Her job sources were generally a referral from a client or a desperate person who couldn't live in chaos one more day. Still, after more than three years, her business remained too sparse to refuse any job.

She didn't have a client, and her dad was out of town so they didn't need her help at his dental clinic. If she didn't take the job, it would be a very lean month.

Like everyone else, she had expenses and if she didn't get a new customer soon she would have to ask her father for a loan. She needed a regular income. Definitely more than the hit and miss work she got with Clutterfree and the few days a month at her dad's clinic.

"Yes, I am."

"Good. I'll check with my son and get back to you. I'd like for him to be here."

So much for her hopes of not seeing Josiah Byrd again. But then she supposed it would be inevitable if she worked for his mother. "Let's say 2:00 p.m. and we can reschedule if he's not available.

Leah spent the next couple of hours preparing for her appointment. She printed the standard contract and reviewed the internet stats she used to help sell her services. She pulled product pamphlets showing items she'd found helpful in organization. Cecily Byrd did not call back.

Before leaving, she checked her email and found her parents had arrived in Spain. Leah knew they planned to visit Barcelona and Madrid. Her mother concluded the note by telling her to be on the lookout for a little gift.

Leah hoped this wasn't an indication of what to expect over the next four weeks. If so, she'd have a collection of trinkets that needed a home and her parents would be bankrupted with shipping costs.

How many times had she told her mother she didn't need trinkets for memories? Maybe she should just place them about her parents' home. Would her mother remember where they came from?

Leah searched the internet for directions to the Byrds' home and found it was in one of the wealthier neighborhoods. She packed her briefcase and dressed in a black pantsuit with a crisp white blouse and black pumps. On her way out, Leah gave herself one last check in the mirror by the door. She looked professional enough. The large silver necklace and earrings her mother had given her last Christmas were the perfect accessory.

Memorial Day was just past and the late spring morning was rather humid. Leah thought they might be in for rain later. She loved spring but the warmer weather made her want to spend her days in air-conditioning. Inside her SUV, she appreciated the full blast of the air conditioner.

Leah arrived in plenty of time for her appointment. Was she too early? She abhorred being late and often erred on the side of being an early bird. She turned into the gated community and stopped at the guardhouse to give her name. The man checked his list, gave her directions and wished her a good day before he opened the gate. Leah admired the beautiful homes as she drove. She spotted the street up ahead and made a left.

Leah parked in the driveway behind Josiah's truck and reached for her briefcase. Getting out, she looked out over the meticulous landscape. They must have a gardener. Nothing like her parents' more casual garden.

She adjusted her jacket and strolled up the sidewalk toward the Byrds' beautiful brick villa.

Josiah pulled the door open as she neared. Leah flashed him a smile. "Hello. I'm so glad you were able to make the appointment."

His anxious appearance combined with his low tone told of his need for discretion. "This isn't my idea. Your card fell out of my coat pocket and Mom found it. If she asks how we met, just make up something about business. Don't mention the letter."

"I wouldn't…"

A petite woman appeared behind him. "Josiah, where are your manners? Don't keep Ms. Wright standing on the porch."

"I just arrived." She leaned around him and reached to shake the woman's hand. "It's a pleasure to meet you, Mrs. Byrd. Please, call me Leah."

His mother led the way to the family room overlooking the Intracoastal Waterway and Wrightsville Beach. From what Leah could see there was no need for her services. The room was beautifully decorated with not a spot of clutter or dust.

"You don't appear to need help."

Cecily laughed and indicated the sofa. "Public rooms. Can't let my guests know what a slob I really am."

"No medicine cabinet sleuths?"

The hoot of laughter from the other woman pleased Leah. "No secrets in the half bath. Just a small first-aid kit and a bottle of aspirin."

Leah grinned. "Perfect. They all envy you your organizational skills and wish they could be the same."

"Have you ever looked into someone else's medicine cabinet?" Cecily Byrd appeared puzzled, as though she had missed out on an obligatory life experience. "I haven't."

Leah sat on the edge of the sofa and placed her briefcase within easy reach. "Not without permission. I don't like intruding on other people's privacy."

Josiah sputtered as though choking and Leah glanced at him.

"Sorry. Must be the pollen."

Not likely, she decided, reading his thoughts loud and clear. "They make great products now to help with that."

"I'll be sure to stop by the drugstore on my way back to the office. Maybe get something for this headache as well."

His mother looked at him. "There's medicine in the upstairs bathroom."

He waved it off. "I'll get something if it doesn't go away."

Leah wasn't deaf to his innuendos. If she was his headache, he'd better buy himself an economy-size bottle of medication.

"Would you care for coffee?" Cecily indicated the beautiful silver service and English bone china cups and saucers on the table.

Leah had already drunk far too many cups that morning. "Thank you, but no. You two go ahead."

"Josiah?"

He accepted the black coffee and sat in an armchair. He stared into the cup as they chatted about the weather.

Cecily placed her cup and saucer on the tray. "Tell me about yourself."

"I'm a local girl. Grew up here in Wilmington and attended college at the university."

"And your parents? Do they live here?"

"Yes, ma'am, they do."

Cecily Byrd showed interest as she continued. "Your last name is Wright? I knew someone named Wright. Now who was it?" She put one finger to her lips. Cecily glanced at Josiah. "I know. He was your father's best friend in high school. They went off to UNC together. For the life of me, I can't remember his first name. I wonder what happened to him."

Leah's breath caught. Surely her father hadn't been Joseph Byrd's best friend. How on earth had he ended up with her mother if she'd been involved with Joseph Byrd? *I don't want to know,* Leah told herself.

She quickly turned the conversation to the reason she was here. "So tell me why you need a clutter consultant?"

Cecily glanced at Josiah and then smiled at Leah. "Mostly I need help clearing my husband's closet. I've been avoiding the task since his death. It's past time but I don't know where to start."

Leah understood. "All those are normal feelings. Avoidance, fear, the need to retreat, holding on to the past, even accepting that you've changed but your world hasn't. How motivated do you consider yourself to be?"

Cecily sighed deeply. "I'm ready."

That sigh told Leah more than Cecily realized. Letting go of her husband's things would be difficult for this woman. "You understand it's not going to be an easy project?"

Cecily's shoulders pushed back indicating her level of determination. "It took a while to collect all these items so it's sure to take even longer to let go of them."

"Good attitude. So many people think they can schedule a couple of hours one afternoon and get it all done."

Cecily laughed heartily at the idea. "Maybe if they're clearing a drawer."

"Exactly." Leah opened her briefcase and pulled out the stats she had found on the internet and liked to share with her clients.

"Did you know the average American receives over forty-nine thousand pieces of mail in their lifetime? And a third of it is junk mail."

Josiah spoke up from his chair. "I don't doubt that. My assistant tosses piles every day."

Leah felt her cheeks warm. Why on earth had she mentioned mail?

"And yet we keep so many papers."

Cecily's comment motivated Leah to continue. She read a couple of random facts. "Eighty percent of what you file is never looked at again. Twenty-five percent of people with two-car garages don't park their cars there. They store their junk."

Josiah and his mother exchanged glances.

"Busted," he said. "Though most of the junk belonged to Dad, I do have a few things out there."

Leah tossed out what she considered to be the most amazing fact. "The storage facility industry is worth a hundred and fifty billion dollars—more than the film business."

"Seriously?" Josiah sat up, showing interest for the first time since she'd arrived.

"Yes. One in eleven American households rents a storage space at a cost of a thousand a year. Not only that, but on average it costs ten dollars a square foot to store items in your home.

"Clutter is a time-waster. Getting rid of it eliminates forty percent of the housework in the average home. As a whole, Americans spend nine million hours a day looking for lost items. And the saddest truth of all is that we spend one whole year of our life looking for lost items."

"Really? A year?"

Leah nodded at Cecily. "So what do you think?"

"I think it would be a worthwhile endeavor." She looked at her son. "Josiah?"

He shrugged and said, "Go for it."

"It takes time and dedication and you have to change the way you think about keeping stuff."

The older woman nodded understanding. "I'm curious, Leah. How did you choose this for a living?"

"Actually I have a bachelor's and I'm working toward my master's but haven't completed my thesis."

She didn't share that her life was on Leah-time and her accomplishments in that area were slow in coming. Her progress had slowed considerably after she'd gotten pneumonia the same summer she completed her coursework. Then the old car her parents had bought her needed work and her dad had offered her a part-time position.

"I also work as a part-time receptionist. One day somewhere between hunting for something I couldn't find and causing a closet landslide I decided I'd had enough. I bagged everything I hadn't worn for a year and knew I'd never wear again and it felt so good I kept going. I read everything I could find on organization and realized people's lives could improve with a few simple principles."

Leah chuckled. "Mom thought I'd lost my mind. She'd spent years trying to train me to put my toys where they belonged, toss the broken stuff and give away the clothes I'd outgrown and here I was all of a sudden getting it. She did warn me about going overboard, though."

A giggle slipped out. "Said I'd better think and rethink my plan since I couldn't afford to replace anything I decided I couldn't live without after it was gone. Anyway, I decided I could do this to help other people and here I am." She grinned broadly. "And now I need to stop talking before you decide I'm fanatical."

Cecily patted her hand. "I think you're very dedicated to what you do."

"Thanks, Mrs. Byrd. I like to think my actions will help someone live a healthier, happier life."

The woman smiled. "I want to work with you."

"Great. I have a standard contract." Leah pulled the folder from her briefcase.

"Let me get my glasses."

After his mother left the room, Leah glanced at Josiah. "Are you okay with this?"

His gaze focused on her, his expression grim. "You're Dad's friend's daughter, aren't you?"

Leah shrugged. "My dad's name is Ben Wright. He and Mom are UNC grads."

"Are both your parents from Wilmington?"

"Dad's family lived here. We moved here because he wanted to be closer to my grandparents and wanted me to know them."

"I suppose he didn't think to look up his old friend when he came back?"

"I can't say if he did or not."

Josiah swept a hand about his neck. "He didn't. Probably best since he was married to your mother who despised my father."

A flash of anger came and went as she decided he looked stressed. "Are you okay?"

"Not really. This mess is like a runaway train. I know I need to get out of the way but I can't. I feel like one of those old cartoons when the villain ties someone to the tracks."

Was he comparing her to a runaway train? Or insinuating she'd restricted him in some way. Either way, his analogy didn't reflect well on her. "Should I leave? Perhaps I can help find someone else to assist your mother."

Josiah shook his head. "It's about what Mom wants. What she needs. It's long past time she got rid of Dad's things. She seems comfortable with you so I'd prefer you stay."

Relief swept through Leah. She needed this job. "We'll start small. In fact, it might be easier for her if you helped with your dad's things. I have a feeling that will be the hardest step for her to take."

"She knows what she wants to keep."

Leah eyed him, noting the way he fidgeted in his chair. Evidently this was something neither Byrd wanted to do. "Does she? A year has passed and she hasn't disposed of the items. Could be she can't let go or is keeping them for you."

Josiah frowned at that. "Dad outweighed me by fifty pounds and his feet were two sizes smaller than mine so I'm not interested in his clothes or shoes. And men aren't like women with jewelry and other stuff."

"What about ties, belts, wallets, briefcases, maybe cuff links? Did he have collectibles you appreciated?"

She could almost see his mind at work. There was something he wanted in this home.

"He had an impressive gun collection."

"Would your mother want you to have that?"

Cecily came back into the room, her glasses hanging on a beaded chain.

"Have what?"

"We were discussing his father's things and he mentioned the gun collection."

Cecily grimaced. "Josiah is more than welcome to those things."

"I don't have space. You sell them and use the money for your new place."

She and her son studied each other. "I have enough money.

You and your father were the ones who appreciated the guns. And you'd have plenty of space if you moved in here."

Leah's gaze moved from one to the other. "Are you planning to leave this house?"

"I'm leasing a condo at Topsail Beach and if I decide to live there permanently I've told Josiah he's welcome to take over this house."

Leah glanced at him. Would they leave this beautiful home empty?

He shrugged. "I have my condo."

"We don't have to decide now," Cecily said. "Even if I buy the smaller place, it'll take time to sort this house out."

"How small are you thinking?"

"At least half the size of this house and all on one floor. A condo."

Leah nodded slowly. The Byrds were talking major downsizing. "How long have you lived here?"

Again Cecily brought one hand up to her lips as she considered the time frame. "Let's see. Nearly eight years. We lived in downtown Wilmington with Joseph's parents after we married and built this house after Joseph's father died."

So Josiah had spent his growing up years in the same house with his parents and grandparents. Leah wondered what it would be like to have three generations living in the same home.

"There's so much in this house. Josiah took a few things to his place and we've donated over the years but the attic is full."

"Well, once you learn organizational skills you'll be able to clear that out."

"We'll see. I'm sure it will require bringing in someone to assess the value of the antiques."

Cecily put on her glasses and picked up the contract. A

few minutes later, she said, "This seems doable. Do you have a pen?"

Leah handed over the engraved gold pen her father had given her for graduation. Cecily signed her name and handed the contract and pen back to her.

"So when do we start?"

"Is tomorrow too soon for you?"

She appreciated the client's readiness to start. "Let's say 9:00 a.m."

Chapter 4

That night, Leah lay in bed thinking of the contract she'd signed. Had she made a mistake? Other than a warning not to mention the letter to his mother, Josiah seemed to have relented when he determined she and his mother got along well together.

Leah still had her doubts. This possibility their fathers might have been best friends at one time and Josiah's ludicrous references to a speeding train didn't bode well for the working relationship. Leah still didn't understand what he'd meant by that.

And of course the situation had snowballed. When he'd walked away on Monday, Leah had been certain she'd seen the last of Josiah Byrd. Now she'd accepted a job with his mother and made plans to start work the next day.

The questions about her parents being from Wilmington made her wonder what Josiah was after. Surely he didn't think her mom had followed his dad here. Or was it because her dad hadn't contacted Joseph Byrd when he returned? Her mother's relationship with Joseph Byrd and subsequent marriage to her father made it seem obvious to Leah that their friendship hadn't survived whatever had happened between her mother and Joseph Byrd.

And while the friendship hadn't been validated, Leah knew almost with certainty that they had been in each other's lives. She wanted to understand the triangle but felt it unlikely that she would. What had Joseph Byrd done to her mother that drove her to write that letter? An angry missive, according to Josiah.

Marty had never discussed her romantic relationships with anyone but Leah's dad. She knew they had started dating in the last semester of their third year of college. Both parents had enjoyed the freedom of living far away from their parents.

Leah's own college experience had been very different. She had lived at home and gone to the University of North Carolina here in Wilmington. UNC by the Sea, as it was sometimes known.

Her days had been filled with classes and hanging out with old and new friends. Occasionally she worked at her dad's dental clinic. She knew he'd been disappointed that she hadn't followed in his footsteps but Leah couldn't make herself choose dentistry as a career. Nor had she wanted to follow in her mother's footsteps and become a bank loan officer. The same job Marty had worked to support her young husband through dental school and provide for their family.

At times, Leah questioned her lack of desire to separate from her parents but she loved them and their relationship was a good one. As a young adult, she'd made her own decisions. They had encouraged her when she'd come up with the plan for her business. She had done well, and when she turned twenty-five and knew it was past time, she found a place of her own and they helped her with the down payment. There had been ups and downs but she managed to pay her bills.

It just seemed that lately she was growing more dissatisfied with the path her life had taken. No regular job, no husband, not even a significant other—nothing promising in her future. The day-to-day existence might be fine for a kid but as an adult woman she felt the need to do something positive with her life.

What had happened to her? Her life had been pretty much close to perfect. Loving, supportive parents had guided her through the stages of growing up and made certain she knew they were proud of her and her accomplishments. Had they ever despaired that she wouldn't achieve the things they hoped for?

One thing for certain, her mother wasn't too thrilled with her at present. With any luck she'd be over this latest faux pas by the time they returned home.

Meanwhile, she needed to take a good look at where she was headed and make changes before it was too late.

Leah awakened before her alarm clock went off at five the next morning and began to formulate her plan for the Byrd organization. Cecily Byrd had said she needed guidance and Leah didn't want to seem unprepared. She turned on the lamp and pulled a legal pad from the nightstand to jot down a few things.

Mrs. Byrd had listed the closet as priority but she had also mentioned the filled attic. And her plan to move into a smaller home. Leah had no idea what the woman intended but if the job took longer than a week or so, she'd welcome the extra work.

She tried to calculate the amount of time the project would take but it wasn't something she could do until she worked with her client. She needed to let Mrs. Byrd set their pace.

Unintentionally Yours

If other jobs came up, Leah would make arrangements with Cecily to work them into the schedule.

After a while Leah gave up on going back to sleep and went into the kitchen to make coffee. The individual cup coffeemaker had been a gift from her parents. When she balked at accepting the expensive gift, they argued that it was cheaper than coffee shops and she could make her coffee fresh with every cup. Both practical considerations for Leah, who loved coffee.

She stood at the window, looking out into the tiny garden. Lights burned here and there but it appeared that most residents were still cozy in their beds.

Leah sipped her coffee and went over to glance at her parents' itinerary. They were in Spain through the fifth. Last time they'd talked, her mother had gone on and on about Madrid. They had eaten churros and visited tapas bars and seen so many beautiful sites. They were moving on to Barcelona today.

She was certain they would make a return visit. Maybe with their adult daughter in tow. Leah laughed at the idea. Who knew? Maybe one day she'd be able to afford such a magnificent trip.

After finishing her coffee, Leah rinsed her cup and turned it over in the drain before heading for the bathroom. She showered and dressed, all the while mentally planning what she would do at the Byrd home. By the time she climbed into her car, she had a general plan but knew enough about planning to understand things often went haywire when others were bought into the picture. She made a stop at her parents' home to fill the water and food bowls, and take Champ for a short walk.

At nine sharp, Cecily opened the door with a smile. "Good morning."

Leah shifted the flat storage boxes she carried. Most clients were never prepared and she liked to have what they needed. "Good morning to you. Ready for a busy day?"

"I think so. Can I help with those?"

Handing over a couple, Leah understood that Cecily would have reservations. So many people were like that. Eager at first and then hesitant when they reconsidered their decision.

"Don't worry. Some of the job may be difficult but once it's done, you'll be glad you did this. In fact, I predict you'll find the work extremely liberating."

Cecily chuckled. "Well, then, let's get started. I'm definitely in need of liberation."

She led the way upstairs and opened a set of beautifully carved doors into one of the most gorgeous rooms Leah had ever seen. "Wow."

Cecily smiled. "I love hearing people say that. I spent a lot of time planning with that reaction in mind."

Leah turned around slowly, taking it all in. The master suite was larger than her condo. There were three doors along the opposite wall and she found herself wondering what was behind door number 1, 2 and 3. "It's perfect. You should be an interior decorator."

"Thank you. I lived in my in-laws' home for many years and could never have things my way. This place was my first opportunity to pull out all the stops and have my dream home."

"It is that." Leah turned back to her. "Okay, what did you want to accomplish first?"

"Well, my primary goal is to empty Joseph's closet. My closet could do with organization as well. And since I'm considering leasing a condo, I need to look at what I want to take with me."

"And you're keeping this house?"

"I'd love it if Josiah married and raised his family here." A smile blossomed over her sweet expression. "And of course kept a guestroom for me when I come to visit my grandchildren."

Leah found herself wondering if Josiah was engaged or involved in a significant relationship. He was a handsome guy and certainly old enough to be considering marriage and fatherhood. "If the other rooms are this size, it would be a mother-in-law suite."

Cecily chuckled. "I love your sense of humor. Josiah isn't exactly on board with the plan. He has a condo and he's not serious about anyone that I know about."

Why did Leah have the feeling her mother shared the same information with her own friends? She knew her parents wanted her to settle down and be happy and it wasn't like she didn't want the same thing, but her list of requirements for her future husband was too long to settle.

She leaned the boxes against the bed. "Let me make a suggestion as to where I think we should start."

On Tuesday night, the phone rang and Leah carefully screwed the lid back on her black nail polish and checked her toes before she reached for the cordless on the sofa pillow next to her.

"Leah?"

Josiah? Why was he calling? She'd had no interaction with him in her first three days of working with Cecily.

"It's Josiah Byrd. I wanted to check in and see how you and Mom are getting along."

Leah doubted that. More likely he wanted to know if she'd spilled the beans about the letter. Or perhaps tied someone to a railroad track. His personality bordered on controlling and if he thought he was going to control her every move, he had another think coming.

"We're getting along just fine. We have been working in

her closet and your mom is motivated. I've had to slow her down a time or two just to be sure she wants to toss so much.

Josiah chuckled. "That's Mom for you. She jumps into every project with both feet."

"Do you jump in with both feet?" Leah had the feeling Josiah was more reserved

About his decisions and things that affected his life.

"I need more time. I like to think things through."

"So this job would take longer if I were working with you?" She groaned silently. Why had she asked that?

"Probably. Listen, about the…I'm sorry if I acted weird about the Dad's friend revelation."

"You seemed stressed."

"I don't want to see my mother hurt."

Leah sighed. How many times did she have to tell him? "I have no intention of hurting Cecily. I didn't want my mom hurt, either. I wish I'd never laid eyes on that stupid letter."

"You and me both. I know you didn't intend… Well, it was an accident but if you slip up while working with Mom, she could be really upset by the truth."

Why did he think the possibility of another woman in his father's youth would upset his mom? Most couples had romantic pasts. What made this one different?

"The letter has nothing to do with our current work agreement. I don't intend to bring it up but that doesn't mean she won't ask my parents' names and if she does I won't lie to her. Lying goes against my beliefs. I would have to tell the truth."

"So truth is more important than hurting people?"

His gruff tone bothered Leah. She wasn't a vicious person. She didn't go around looking for truths to expose so she could make people cry. "That's not what I said. I think you're trying to make a big deal out of nothing. Besides, you're the one who dropped my business card in her house."

"You could have said you were busy."

Easy for him to say. He had money. "Unfortunately, I can't afford to turn down any job that comes my way. I have bills to pay and your mother wants my help. I think we're both adult enough to handle this."

Josiah issued a weary sigh. "Maybe it was meant to be. Where would Mom be without you now?"

More than likely right where she was when they started. "Wanting to change things and not knowing how?"

He grunted in agreement. "I'm depending on you to keep our secret."

"There is no secret, Josiah. All I know is my mother wrote a letter to your father."

"Surely you have suspicions."

Leah disliked the fine edge to his tone. "What exactly bothers you so much about that letter?"

"You should have read it."

It had nothing to do with her, or him, for that matter. So what if their parents had dated in their youth? They had married other people and moved on with their lives.

"It's not a big deal, Josiah. People date. Relationships go sour."

"You don't know the whole story."

And she probably never would, but Leah was okay with that. "Neither do you. You read Mom's point of view. Surely you've had arguments before. It's the past. We don't get do-overs. We move on. Forgive and forget."

"Hard to forget things like wives and unwanted babies."

Leah shook her head. What was he talking about? All his obscure references were enough to drive a person crazy. Who was unwanted? Never mind. It wasn't her concern. "When do you plan to come over and help with your dad's things?"

"Can't you just pack up his clothes and give them away?"

Leah thought about how she'd feel if this were her dad. She'd do this for him and her mom. "Is that really what you want? He was your father. Don't you feel you owe him and your mother this little thing?"

Leah's relationship with her father had always been a good one. She'd been her daddy's little princess. Oh, he chastised her when the need arose, even paddled her when she'd really misbehaved, but Leah knew the spankings had hurt him more than her. She felt remorse for forcing him to take action. He'd never struck her in anger or without explanation. He discussed the whys of his decision and never left her in doubt about his choices.

Her parents had given her everything, not just material possessions but morals and values. They'd taken her to church and had been there when she accepted Jesus into her heart. She'd grown to appreciate their parenting skills and hoped to one day utilize those skills with her children.

"Leah? You there?"

"Yes." She dragged herself back to their conversation.

"I said I'll take care of it on Thursday. Mom has lunch with her friends so let's do it then. Get his things out of the house before she comes home."

"It would be easier. But you should tell her what you plan. See if she has any objections or if there's anything she needs to keep. I can tell her what we plan tomorrow if you'd like."

"No. I'll talk to her. See what she's thinking."

"That's probably best. She's held on to his things for a year. There's something holding her back."

"It's all she has left of him. Once they're gone she'll be forced to move on. I tell her she doesn't need them. That she has the memories."

Leah hoped they were good memories. She liked Cecily. "You really don't want to do this, do you?"

"Not really," Josiah said. "That's the pitfall of being an only child. If I'd had a sister, she could help Mom. She'd be more understanding. Men aren't equipped to care about things. I'd toss the lot without looking at anything."

The statement both horrified and fascinated her. "You actually admit to that?"

"I'll deny it if you tell anyone."

Leah laughed at his hasty disavowal. "Think of me as your sister. It's my job to help Cecily get through this without a great deal of regret."

"I do appreciate your efforts. I've talked with Mom a couple of times since you've started and she seems different. She's made so many changes recently."

"Does that bother you?"

Why did she keep asking him these leading questions? She needed to stop. It wasn't her job to analyze him.

"It's not something I think about often but she's not so old in the scheme of things. She needs to do the things that make her happy."

"My parents are only slightly older and they're both so vital and active I don't even try to keep up with them."

"You say they're on a trip?"

Leah immediately warmed to the subject. "Second honeymoon. You should have seen Mom's face. Daddy has never done anything like this. She was thrilled."

"Sounds like you are, too."

"Oh yes, I hoped he'd do something wonderful and he did."

She heard the phone beep and knew he had an incoming call. "That's Mom calling. Gotta run. I'll plan on seeing you Thursday. I'll let you know if anything changes."

"Okay. Good night, Josiah."

When Leah ended the call, Josiah said into the phone, "Hey, Mom. I was just thinking about you. How do you feel about me taking you out to dinner tomorrow night?"

"That would be lovely."

"I'll pick you up around six. Any place in particular?"

"I've been craving seafood."

"Seafood it is. Something on your mind?"

"I just remembered your dad's friend's name. It was Ben. They played football together."

Leah's dad. Josiah rubbed his forehead. "Why are you thinking about that, Mom?"

"It bugged me. I should have remembered. He dated one of my girlfriends. He was a nice guy. I remember asking Joseph once if he ever heard from Ben and he said something about him not being much of a friend. I thought it strange considering they had been friends since the first grade."

"Maybe Dad felt that way because they lost touch."

"As far as I know he never tried to contact Ben after he came home from Chapel Hill. It wouldn't have been difficult since his parents lived right here in the city. They could have told him how to get up with their son."

Probably more difficult than she realized, Josiah thought. He doubted his father wanted anything to do with the woman he'd deceived or his former best friend after he learned they were married.

"I'll have to ask Leah what her dad's name is tomorrow. Wouldn't it be delightful if it were Ben?"

Her enthusiasm made Josiah wonder exactly what his mom was thinking. "Did you have a crush on this guy or something?"

She laughed at his question. "Oh, no, nothing like that. I only had eyes for Joseph. It makes the world seem smaller when we connect with people from our past through others. Don't you find it intriguing that Leah could be your father's friend's daughter?"

Josiah defined his reaction as frightened rather than intrigued. Ever since he'd initiated their first meeting, he'd had a feeling the truth would come out and didn't know how to stop it from happening.

He could only hope his mother would forget again but somehow he didn't think his luck would hold. Should he warn Leah? Give her the opportunity to get her story together? No, he decided. It would be more natural if she were surprised by the news.

The following evening, Josiah pulled out his mother's chair and waited until she was settled before going around to his own seat. "Did you make good progress today?"

Cecily shook out the napkin and settled it across her lap. "Some. We're still working in my closet. When we had the house plans drawn up, your father insisted on his own closet. Said he was tired of digging through my things to find his. I'm beginning to understand what he meant.

"I never realized how much was in there. Leah joked about possessions growing to meet the available space and mine certainly have."

Josiah shrugged thoughtfully. "Maybe we're all hoarders by nature."

They paused to give the waiter their drink and food orders. He returned a few minutes later with the iced tea and a basket of hush puppies.

Josiah blessed the food and munched on one of the crispy, fried, corn bread pieces. "I'm going over to work with Leah on Thursday while you're at lunch with your friends. We're going to empty Dad's closet."

She didn't speak.

"You know it's time, don't you, Mom?"

Cecily took a sip of water. "It's hard, Josiah. We were together for so long. I feel so alone."

He wanted to say she wasn't alone, that she had him. But that wouldn't be fair. He knew his mother loved him. She'd proven that love so many times in her lifetime. But the love she held for his father had been different, the type of love he had yet to experience, the intimacy of man and wife.

Josiah traded the thought for something he'd told Leah. "You have the memories, Mom. No one can take those away. Do you really need the clutter?"

She fiddled with the silverware. "After Joseph died I used to stand in his closet and breathe in his scent. Gradually it went away. Then I'd touch his clothes and remember how he looked in them. How it felt to make sure he left the house perfectly dressed every day. You know how he was about that. I was so proud of him. He was a very handsome man."

"You have the photos."

"Too many. Leah has suggested I gather them all into one place so I can get them organized for storage."

"Aren't they in photo albums?"

"Some are. Others are in drawers and boxes. Don't forget, I have both sets of grandparents' photos as well as ours. Leah said I might want to take up scrapbooking as a hobby. I might consider that. Though I'd need a library for all the books."

He took another hush puppy. "Back to the closet."

"The clothes will serve a better purpose helping those in need."

"You could put them in a consignment shop. They were expensive."

She waved off the idea. "I'd rather donate them. I thought about Hank at the office. He and your father were about the same size."

Josiah frowned. "I don't know, Mom. He might not be comfortable wearing Dad's clothes."

"And you wouldn't be comfortable seeing him and knowing they were your father's?"

She'd hit the bull's-eye with that one. Josiah shook his head.

"We'll give them to the men's shelter. They have men looking for work who need clothes."

"Have you removed your must-keeps?"

She nodded. "A few things. You will remember to check his pockets? He was the worst for cramming things in his pockets."

At the sight of her misty gaze, Josiah reached over to squeeze her hand. "We will."

"And keep something for yourself." Her sad eyes pleaded with him. "You may think you don't want anything now but one day you'll wish you had kept something."

"I'll take care of it. Here comes our food. This restaurant has the best broiled shrimp."

They ate in silence for a few minutes before his mother said, "Oh, I forgot to tell you. Leah's father is Ben Wright. Isn't that amazing? He lives right here in Wilmington and has a dental practice. Can you believe it? All these years he's been right here in the same city. I wish your father had known."

Josiah thought he probably had but had kept the information to himself. Had he avoided them because the temptation to get back with Martha Wright would have been too strong? He knew what it felt like to be cheated on and was thankful his mother hadn't experienced the same.

"Leah said her parents are on a second honeymoon. I told her we'd have to get together when they returned. I can't wait to see Ben again. It's been ages."

Not long enough, Josiah thought.

Chapter 5

Leah glanced up when Josiah walked into the bedroom. "Your mom left a few minutes ago."

"I had an appointment. I tried to get here before she left." He shed his suit coat and unbuttoned the sleeves of his light blue dress shirt. When his efforts to roll them failed, Josiah extended his arms toward Leah. "Give me a hand, here. I should have brought a change of clothes."

She smoothed the sleeves back in neat folds. "There. You'll be fine. It's not hot or dusty in this house."

Leah had the doors of his father's closet open and Josiah pushed at the familiar suits arrayed before him. "Seems so impersonal to see them en masse like this. More like a clothing store."

"I'm sure you have memories of him wearing them."

He nodded and fingered the rich fabric of the black wool suit closest to him. "Dad was a stickler for being well dressed. Everything in the most current style, clean and pressed, with snow-white shirts and shined shoes. He believed clothes made the man."

Leah glanced over her shoulder at him. "Is that what you believe?"

"Appearance does play a major role in the way we're perceived by others but there are other aspects. Dad said people rarely got to know the real man, but they did business with those who impressed them. But I believe a man's reputation is more important. If he's not trustworthy, no one is going to bother with the outward show."

Leah admired his confidence. He spoke as though he could care less what others thought. She pulled at her top. "Guess he wouldn't be impressed by me."

She blushed when Josiah gave her the once-over. The denim capris and white T-shirt had seemed the perfect outfit that morning.

"You're dressed appropriately for your work. And you were impressive that first day you came here for the appointment."

Leah chuckled. "This is the real me. I'm a casual kind of person."

He raised one dark eyebrow. "As opposed to a stuffed shirt like me?"

She surprised him by bursting into a fit of giggles. "Sorry. I couldn't help myself. Every time I hear that phrase I get this image of a turkey in a button-down shirt. Truly, you wear your clothes well." Then she blushed and grimaced as she looked away and muttered, "Awkward." Where had that come from? No one had said anything about his appearance.

"Not at all. I'm glad you appreciate the *GQ* aspect of my wardrobe. But for the record, I have plenty of grunge wear at home."

They stared at each other a few seconds longer before

Leah turned to the closet. "Let's get started. Cecily will be back in a couple of hours."

"She cautioned me at least a half-dozen times to check all his pockets. He was always tucking bits and pieces in them."

Leah nodded. "She said the same to me. I bought these suit boxes but forgot to get hangers."

He shrugged and took a suit from the closet rail, leaving it on the wood hanger. "Use these. Mom can buy more if she needs them."

They made good progress, removing change and the occasional receipt from the pockets. Josiah studied one that was more than a year old. "This drove our office manager crazy. She'd call Mom and ask her to check his pockets for receipts. He wouldn't stop no matter how many times Liz told him he had to turn them in. I guess she let this one slide after he died. Probably didn't want to upset Mom."

Leah pushed her hand into a pants pocket and pulled out a pocketknife.

"You might want this."

He put down the suit he held and took the knife, turning it over in his hands a couple of times. "Dad always carried this."

She left Josiah to his private moment and opened a dresser drawer. Starched white shirts, neatly folded, were stacked there. Leah noted that Josiah pocketed the knife and reached for the suit.

"What's the plan for these clothes?"

"Mom mentioned the men's shelter."

"That's good. She can get a tax donation receipt. Church clothes closets are good, too. So many people come in looking for clothes."

"I'm sure she'd be okay with you taking some to your church."

Leah shook her head. "Cecily doesn't need to rethink this. She's having a hard enough time as it is."

He nodded, his expression grim. "Mom insists I keep something of Dad's but his clothes and shoes don't fit, not that I'd feel comfortable wearing them if they did. They would be a constant reminder of him."

Leah wondered why he didn't want to be reminded of his father. "What about some of the ties you gave him?"

He glanced at her. "How do you know I gave him ties?"

"While there are kids who never had the privilege, you strike me as the kind of son who gave the man who already had everything special ties."

Josiah sniffed at that. "Bet you can't tell which ones."

She met his challenge. "Oh ye of little faith. Watch and learn."

Leah walked over to the tie holder. "Ooh, nice gadget. You should keep this for your ties."

"I have one. Christmas gift from Mom."

She hit the button that moved the ties around. "I'll have to find one for my dad. He'd like it."

"Take that one."

She looked at him and frowned. Why was he being so offhand with his father's possessions? "I couldn't."

"Mom wouldn't care. I certainly wouldn't."

Leah busied herself with the ties. "You're trying to side-track me."

Josiah moved to sit in an armchair and waved his hand for her to continue.

"Definitely this one." She held up a cartoon character tie.

"Too easy."

"I'm just getting started."

He watched closely as she fingered them, slipping the occasional tie from the rack and placing it on the bed. When she finished, Leah waved an arm over the bed. "Am I right?"

Josiah stood and reviewed her choices. His eyes narrowed, squinting at her. "How did you do it?"

Satisfied that she'd achieved her goal, Leah said, "Easy. Your dad leaned toward a specific style. These newer styles, colors, patterns, et cetera, are ties that appeal to a younger man."

"I chose ties I thought he'd like." She heard the defensiveness in his tone.

Leah nodded, her ponytail flipping from over her shoulder. "And I'm sure he did, though like most men he had his favorites and far more than he could wear. Cecily's choices have a more masculine yet feminine appeal."

"She was always telling him to change his tie because it had a stain. Same reason I keep a replacement tie in my desk drawer. They're stain magnets."

Leah looked at him expectantly. "So what do you think? Do you want to keep any of them?"

He walked over to the closet and removed another tie from the rack. "I'll take this one. I always liked it." He moved back to the bed and picked up three more. "And these."

Leah nodded approval. "Now you can tell your mom you chose something."

"Let's keep going."

By the time Cecily returned, his father's closet and dresser drawers were empty. They had discarded a few pieces but had a large collection of items to be donated.

Cecily beamed. "Thanks, Leah."

She waved a hand at Josiah. "Thank your son."

Cecily took Josiah's hand and looked up at him. "I'm sure she made the task as easy for you as she has for me."

"She did. Plus she picked out the ties I gave Dad. I still don't know how."

Cecily laughed. "Well, son, your dad always picked the same style ties."

"He had more style than me. I kept one of his ties. And

his pocketknife, if you don't mind. Leah found it in a pants pocket."

Cecily sighed in relief. "Yes, that's good. I can't tell you how glad I am that this is done. I've dreaded it for so long and you two have lifted the burden from my shoulders. And Josiah, your dad would be thrilled to know you have his knife. It was your grandfather's."

Leah saw the sadness that overwhelmed Josiah.

"Don't do this, Mom."

"Your father loved you, Josiah."

He glanced at Leah and she saw something in his eyes she couldn't quite make out.

Josiah took a step toward the door. "I have to get back to work."

Cecily reached out to him. "Please stay, Josiah. We need to talk."

He shook his head, refusing to look at her. "Not now."

As he all but ran from the room, Leah felt guilty. She knew everyone had to deal with their grief in their own way and the idea that she might have caused him even more suffering hit her hard. Before she could think, Leah said, "I'll talk to him."

She paused long enough to grab his coat and hurried after Josiah. She caught his elbow. "Don't be like this."

He shook her hand off. "You don't understand, Leah."

"Then help me. What's going on?"

"He wouldn't care."

"You mean about the things you kept?"

He crossed his arms over his chest. "Yeah, Dad never really cared about anything I did. Mom said he didn't know how to love but he obviously knew how to love your mom."

Angry, Leah snapped, "You don't know that. And since they didn't get together, I'd say it wasn't a love match."

"I read the letter. You didn't."

She was sick of hearing about that stupid letter. "You read

a young woman's angry comments. You only know a little bit of one side of the story."

He shoved his hands over his head as if trying to brush the memory away. "I know they would be together if not for me."

"Really, Josiah?" Her sarcastic tone spoke volumes. "Aren't you giving yourself a lot of credit?"

Confused, he stared at her. "Why would you ask that?"

"You weren't even born. Just how did you change your father's life?"

He wouldn't look at her. "I was conceived."

Leah shook her head. "You didn't make his decisions. If he'd been serious about Mom, do you really think he'd have risked losing her?"

He didn't respond. "Let me answer that for you. No, Josiah, he wouldn't have. No matter how tempted he might have been, he would have made a different choice. And while his decisions hurt more people than him it is not your fault, not your mom's or my mom's, either. Life is about choices and he was wrong to hurt you.

"And if you let these crazy thoughts ruin your life, you're even more wrong than he was. Don't carry on that legacy."

"Isn't that what started this? Mom's desire for me to keep something of his?"

Leah understood the underlying problem hadn't just started today. Josiah had carried this burden for a long time. "I don't know what kind of relationship you had with your dad but he was the only father you'll ever have and you really should push past the negatives and embrace the positives."

His look was incredulous. "Positives? Oh, yeah, I'll be sure to embrace them. Just as soon as I think of one." His sarcasm ripped into her as he all but shouted the words. "Is this part of your job, Leah?"

"Stop it, Josiah. It's just friendly advice. Look around you."

She turned and waved her arm about. "I'd say your parents did right by you. They provided this gorgeous home…"

"I never lived here. I'd already left home and moved into my condo when they built this house. The only family home I ever knew was my grandparents' home downtown and dad couldn't get rid of it fast enough after my grandfather died. This house was more prestigious. More fitting for a wealthy businessman like him."

The distaste in his tone unsettled her. "Well, he made sure you got an education and provided for your future with the business. If he hadn't loved you, do you truly believe he would have done all that? You think he couldn't have walked away just as so many other men have done?"

Josiah shook his head, a stubborn frown setting his mouth. "I wish he had but my grandparents wouldn't have let him. They believed in doing the right thing."

"What would they have done? Dragged him back and held him at gunpoint until he married your mom? I don't believe for a second that Cecily would have wanted him that way. Your dad loved your mom and accepted his responsibilities. And she loved him."

He stepped away from her. "Just stop, Leah. I'm not one of your projects. You can't compartmentalize my life."

"That's not what I'm trying to do."

"Yes, you are. Ever since we met you have been stirring things up and I don't like it. Not one bit."

He grabbed the coat she held and the door slammed shut behind him, leaving her glad he hadn't shattered the beautiful glass inset in his anger.

Leah turned to find Cecily coming down the stairs. Her hopeful look evaporated with the shake of Leah's head. "I'm sorry to pull you into our drama."

"I signed on for the job."

Cecily shook her head. "Not playing referee between us, you didn't."

"I asked him to help with the closet. I don't understand. What set him off like that?"

She looked sad. "I'm pretty sure it was my comment about his father being happy that pushed him over the edge. Josiah gets touchy when I say his dad loved him."

Leah recognized that to be a fact. "Why?"

"Let's get a glass of iced tea and I'll tell you."

She followed Cecily into the kitchen and leaned against the island as the woman filled crystal goblets with ice from the fridge door and removed a matching pitcher from inside. She poured the golden brew into both glasses. "It's sweet. Is that okay?"

Cecily added lemon slices and Leah grinned as she accepted the glass. "Is there any other way?"

"Let's sit on the deck. It's nice out today."

They settled on comfortable loungers and looked out over the waterway as they sipped in silence.

Cecily's voice was low as she spoke. "To help you understand Josiah's problems, I need to share the past. I suppose most people would say Joseph was a very self-centered man. He worked hard for the things he wanted and that made him appear selfish.

"When he was in high school, his father didn't think Joseph needed to attend college. Jim had a high school diploma and a successful real estate business. He decided Joseph could do the same. But Joseph wanted to escape his father's home. He played football and got a scholarship. He told his father it was stupid to reject a free education and Jim reluctantly agreed, so after graduation, Joseph went off to Carolina."

Cecily shifted uncomfortably in her seat. "I didn't hear from him often but when I did, all he could talk about was how much he enjoyed being on his own. Then he'd feel guilty and say that I could come there, too, when I graduated. He always told me he loved me before we hung up. It was enough to hold me until his next phone call."

"You didn't date anyone else?"

She shook her head. "No one ever asked. They knew I was Joseph's girl. He came home that summer to work for his dad and it was just like old times except that we didn't have to sneak around to see each other. My parents finally agreed I could date. I'd missed him and was so happy he was home. But all too soon summer ended and he went away again.

"It was my senior year and I was excited by the possibilities. That spring when my prom came up, I pleaded with him and Joseph promised he would come home that weekend to escort me.

"My parents agreed that I could spend the night with my girlfriends and, well, Joseph and I made a decision that changed the path of our future." She blushed with the admittance.

"He went back to college to finish out the year and my head was filled with thoughts of that night, graduation, and completing college paperwork. And then I realized Josiah was on the way. I needed to tell Joseph and my parents but decided to wait until he came home so we could tell them together."

Leah considered how frightened Cecily must have been and her decision to wait to share the news.

"It was only a couple of months but I hadn't counted on my mom's eagle eye. She figured it out before I could tell her. Then she told my dad and they confronted me. Dad told Joseph's parents and things escalated out of control.

"Next thing I knew, Josiah is back home and we're sitting on the love seat at the Byrds' home listening to all four parents tell us what we were going to do.

"As far as they were concerned, we'd made one wrong decision and they had no intention of allowing us to make

another. We would be married in May after Joseph finished
out the school year. Joseph would finish college here at home.
His parents had the larger house so they decided we would
live with them until Joseph could provide us with a home.

"His father wanted him to go to work right away but my
parents argued that he would be a better provider with a college education. They offered to pay for his last two years. I'll
never forget how Jim Byrd made some comment about his
son being a lucky boy and managing to get his free education
despite his stupidity. That really hurt Joseph."

He had hurt Cecily, too, Leah thought.

"I finished high school but there was no college for me.
Maxine Byrd wasn't in the best of health so I managed the
house and took care of her and Josiah after he was born."

"You took care of your mother-in-law?"

Cecily nodded. "She had breathing problems. Josiah
adored her. He still misses his grandmother."

"But not his father and grandfather?"

"Joseph and Josiah did not have a typical father-son relationship. Joseph was always too busy or too tired to be bothered by the little boy who idolized him. I did everything I
could to encourage Joseph to provide a positive and loving environment but he didn't. Josiah had no foundation to grow on.

"By the time Josiah's teen years rolled around, it was too
late. The two of them couldn't be in the same room without
arguing. Joseph had the talk with Josiah and told him we'd
made a mistake. Josiah didn't take that well. He decided his
father hated him. He did some things that nearly got him in
over his head but then he settled down, graduated and opted
to attend UNC. I don't know if it was to impress or infuriate
his father. Joseph resented not being able to finish his education there."

His education or his dating? Leah's heart hurt for Cecily.

Choices had changed her life, her dreams and hopes, and had turned her into a parent and caregiver far too soon in life.

"Don't feel sorry for me, Leah. Josiah changed my world in the best way. I love him with all my heart and he's worth far more to me than everything I gave up. It just breaks my heart to know he's hurting and I can't reach him. Most of the time he's fine but then I try to reconcile the relationship with his dad and he loses it. I wish he could let go but he can't."

Leah considered the lack of decisions she'd made in her life. She'd moved out and started Clutterfree but knew she could always fall back on her parents if she failed. Or maybe *when,* if things kept going like they had lately. With this job she was solvent, but what would she do when it ended?

She wouldn't think about that now. Her life was in God's hands and she believed He would direct her path. She believed He had a plan for her just as He did for Josiah and Cecily and they all had to wait on God's timing.

And yet she'd managed to hurt Josiah Byrd again. "I shouldn't have asked him to help me with the closet. I was thinking of you and thought it would make things easier but apparently it only made things worse."

Cecily reached over to pat her hand. "No more than usual. The positive in all this is that he helped you despite his unwillingness."

Leah didn't exactly see Josiah's reaction as a positive.

"I think we should call it a day. That closet was a major task and I'm sure you're ready for a rest."

"I need to finish labeling the boxes and move them out of your bedroom."

"We'll handle it together."

They rose and walked to the door. "And Leah, I am sorry you got caught up in this."

Like the story with Josiah and his father, there was another story Cecily didn't know. A story that involved Leah that couldn't be shared.

"Not a problem. We said it wasn't going to be easy when we started. We'll get through this together."

Cecily linked arms with her. "We will."

Chapter 6

Leah felt out of sorts as she looked over the items Cecily had pulled out of the hall closet. She'd worked another job that morning with a lady who wanted a half day of closet sorting. Cecily had given her the go-ahead since she had doctor appointments.

But Leah's thoughts weren't on her work. Early that morning she had gone by to check on her parents' pets and found Champ listless with no appetite. She called their vet and he said the dog might be missing her parents and suggested he stay at the clinic overnight as a precaution.

Then the other client said she'd had enough after two hours of work. They had barely scratched the surface but she insisted on quitting so they did.

It had been after one by the time she and Cecily settled in to work on the hall closet and they hadn't made much progress. Cecily wandered along the memories pathway many times, insisting she couldn't dispose of the things they found there.

Leah despaired when the woman opened a scrapbook and fingered an old dried-up corsage. "Joseph gave me this for my senior prom. I've had it since I was seventeen years old."

"Is there a photo of you wearing the corsage?"

Cecily smoothed a finger over the edges. "A Polaroid. It was a special night."

"Why don't we put the scrapbook in the keep/think about pile?"

That same pile had become their biggest by the time the afternoon passed. It was getting late when the doorbell rang. Cecily went to answer while Leah tossed trash into bags. She couldn't imagine how they had managed to fill two bags after keeping so many things but they had. She heard Cecily talking to someone who sounded like Josiah.

"Leah, dear, can you come to the kitchen?"

She stood and brushed off her clothes, tucking her hair behind her ears. She'd worn it down that day.

It was Josiah. He stood at the kitchen island. A couple of brown bags with delicious smells emanating from them rested on the countertop.

Leah felt self-conscious when his gaze came to rest on her face. "Hi. I surprised Mom with Chinese takeout but she has other plans."

"You should have called. Why don't you and Leah dine together?" She turned to Leah and asked, "Did you have plans for dinner?"

Feeling awkward, Leah shook her head. She hadn't thought that far ahead. Most nights she picked up a salad or made herself a sandwich out of whatever she had in the fridge. "No, ma'am."

Cecily couldn't have looked more pleased with herself if she'd preplanned their evening. "There you go, Josiah. You can share this wonderful meal with this beautiful young woman and neither of you will dine alone."

"Mom…"

"I couldn't."

His protest and her refusal came out at the same time.

"Nonsense." Cecily glanced at Leah. "You've had a difficult day. The least my son can do is feed you."

Josiah showed concern. "What happened?"

"I had to leave Champ at the vet's office. He's off his food and won't move. I haven't heard from them yet."

"I'm sorry. Mom's right. Please stay and share this meal with me. Let's say it's a peace offering for the way I acted last Thursday."

Cecily smiled and wrapped an arm about her son's waist. "Those are my favorite words."

Josiah hugged her closer. "What's that?"

"Why, 'Mom's right' and 'I'm sorry,' of course."

He shook his head. "I can be a jerk at times. And Mom, I don't say those words often enough. Where are you going tonight?"

She looked up at him. "Shopping with Carol. I promised to help her pick out clothes for a cruise she's taking. We've both been busy and she leaves for Florida next week. This is the only time I have."

"You could eat with us before you go."

"We're going for a salad after we finish. She wants to share her itinerary and I want to catch up with what's been going on in her life."

"Okay, Mom. Leah will eat your hot and sour soup. They made it just the way you like."

"Oh." Slight disappointment flitted over her features. "You'll love it, Leah."

Leah smiled, still trying to find an escape. She couldn't claim she needed to go home to the pets. Lady was so self-sufficient she didn't need humans for more than food and cleaning her litter box. "We can put it in the fridge for later."

Cecily shook her head. "It's best eaten right away. You have to try it. I tell Josiah all the time that he doesn't know what he's missing."

Josiah's smile was sympathetic. "Just give in, Leah. You've already told her you don't have plans."

She flushed. "Okay. I'll be happy to eat Cecily's hot and sour soup. It's my favorite, too."

Cecily glanced at her watch. "Look at the time. I need to freshen up before I go."

Leah started to follow. "I need to finish cleaning that mess we've made outside the closet."

"Leave it. We'll just have to pull everything back out tomorrow." Cecily kissed Josiah's cheek and then Leah's.

"Have fun." Again they spoke in unison.

The unity continued as they pulled plates from the cabinets and Leah filled glasses with ice and tea. Josiah found silverware and napkins. "Sorry. I didn't get chopsticks."

"That's okay. I never could figure out how to eat soup with them."

He grinned at her tongue-in-cheek comment and she grinned back just as Cecily popped in to say good-night. His mother wore a pleased expression on her face as she went through the mudroom into the garage.

"I'm glad she's going out. She's lonely."

He nodded. "She is. It's the reason she's making so many changes in her life."

He poured the soup into a bowl and set it on the island. "Don't wait on me. Eat while the soup is hot." He slid a packet of fried noodles over to her.

Leah picked up the soup spoon. "What makes this so special?"

"Mom declares it's got the best flavor she's ever eaten. She asks for green onions and extra noodles."

"Would you say grace?"

Josiah came over to the island and took her hand in his. He asked God's blessings on the food they were about to eat and thanked Him for providing a friend with whom to enjoy the evening meal.

His words filled Leah with warmth. She'd been attracted to Josiah when they first met but never imagined they would see each other again.

"I'm sorry about the way I acted the other day. I was wrong."

"Not if that's the way you feel. You should have told me you weren't comfortable and I shouldn't have pushed you so hard. I just wanted to save Cecily the pain of doing it."

Josiah nodded. "I know your intentions were good. Unfortunately you got caught up in one of my moments and I apologize. I have plenty of fried rice and chicken." He sat the second bag on the island and removed two cartons, one small and one larger. Another small paper package contained egg rolls. "They're shrimp."

Josiah served his plate and pushed the containers in Leah's direction. She placed a spoon of the meat and vegetable dish and one of the egg rolls on her plate. Their shoulders bumped when he took the seat next to hers.

"I meant for you to eat the rest."

"No way. The soup and egg roll will fill me up." She brought another spoonful to her mouth. "Your mom is right. This is wonderful."

They ate in silence until Leah asked, "How was work today?"

"Showed a couple of properties, a few inquiries about listings and one sale. What about you?"

"Cecily had appointments so I took the morning off to do another job. My client wasn't as motivated. Then this situation with Champ."

"How old is he?"

"Fourteen. Mom thought Queen Elizabeth's corgis were so cute she wanted her own. I know he's old but I pray the vet's right and he's missing Mom and Dad. It would be horrible if something happened."

"Where are they?"

"On their way to London. Mom raved about how romantic Paris was."

She noted the way Josiah watched her so closely. "Would you like to see Paris?"

"Oh, yes, definitely. I hope to travel extensively. Once I get my finances in order and can afford to. Right now, buying a tank of gas to drive around Wilmington is about the most travel I can afford."

Josiah chuckled. "I'd bike to work but I don't think my clients would be willing to ride on the handlebars. I take it the organization business took a hit with the economy?" He forked food into his mouth and chewed.

"Yes. Another luxury in lean times."

"Maybe you should specialize in helping people raise funds with their excess junk."

Leah shrugged. It was a thought. Would her clientele increase if she helped turn their excess into dollars. "I have helped a few get their items up on eBay and they've done well. Some have had yard sales and we often list curbside items on Craigslist."

"No curbside here."

"We could always leave it up at the guardhouse."

Josiah laughed at her teasing grin. "I don't even want to think what the association would do with that." He tapped the carton with his fork. "Sure you don't want more of this?"

"I'm stuffed. You eat it."

He stirred around in the container, eating bits and pieces. "Here you go." Josiah tossed her a fortune cookie.

Leah broke it open and read. "Ooh, changes in my future. What does yours say?"

He frowned as he read. "Where do they get this stuff?"

She bumped his shoulder. "Come on. What does it say?"

"I'm going to find love in the place I least expect it."

Leah frowned. "Does that mean you have to go someplace to find love?"

Josiah shrugged. "I have no idea."

She stood and stacked her dishes, taking them over to the sink. Josiah followed. "You bought dinner. I'll do the dishes," she said.

"Okay. I'll take out the garbage. Tomorrow is trash day."

Leah remembered the bags in the hallway upstairs. "I need to get our trash. It's heavy and I don't want Cecily lugging those bags around."

"I'll get them."

Not wanting to risk Josiah tossing some of Cecily's keep items, Leah went upstairs with him. She separated the bags from the piles in the hallway.

Josiah pointed to the huge pile sitting off to the side. "What about that?"

She shook her head quickly. "That's Cecily's 'think about' pile. It stays until she makes her final decision."

He looked at it again. "What's in there?"

"Lots of things. A scrapbook she kept in high school. Some letters your dad wrote to her."

"Junk." He flapped his hand in dismissal.

"Young woman's treasures."

Unconvinced, he said, "It's still junk."

Leah eyed him. "Don't you have anything like that?"

"If I do, I'm sure it's in this house. Even if I wanted to toss the stuff, Mom wouldn't let me. She's big on keeping things for the future."

"And we're big on throwing memories away with both hands."

Even as she spoke the words, Leah didn't know why the thought came to mind. Cecily and Marty fought to keep the things they hoped their children would one day treasure. "Maybe they know something we don't know."

Josiah's head tilted as he looked doubtful. "What could holding on to the past possibly mean to anyone?"

Leah knew he would have the answer to his problems with his father if he could answer that question.

"I'm sure Cecily wants to show your kids pictures of their dad as a kid. They'll laugh at the things they don't recognize due to technological advances and you'll do your best to convince them it was the best thing ever made."

"By the time I have kids, CDs and MP3 players will be antiques. Technology is moving at the speed of sound. I can't even keep up."

"I know, but maybe we should listen to our parents and not be so hasty about discarding things."

"That's strange coming from an organization expert. Isn't it your job to get the stuff out of their lives?"

He had a point. No one would hire a consultant who only directed them to rid themselves of a couple of items. "Maybe not all of it. I think I need to stop fighting Cecily and listen to why things are important to her. Then help her develop a way to find those items when she feels the need to see them."

He shook his head. "Well, I'm taking these bags down before Mom goes through them and decides she can't live without this stuff."

"You think she will?" That perplexed Leah. It had never occurred to her that Cecily might reconsider the decisions made each day.

"Out of sight, out of mind."

"Oh, Josiah…" Before she could continue her cell rang.

She tugged it from her pocket and looked at the caller ID. The vet's office. "Hello," she said, holding her breath with the surge of fear.

"Hi, Leah, Kevin Parker. I hate to call you so late but I thought you might want to know that Champ…"

"Is he okay? Has something happened?" Fear tinged her voice.

"I'm sorry, Leah. Champ didn't make it. I thought that might be the case earlier when you told me how he was acting. I knew your parents were out of town and didn't want you having to deal with this alone."

"Champ's…dead?"

"I'm really sorry, Leah. I know how much you loved him."

Leah could hardly think. She sank to her knees, rocking back and forth as she cried for her old friend.

"Leah? What is it? What's happened?"

"Champ… He…"

She couldn't get the words past the lump in her throat.

Josiah dropped the bags and knelt to pull her into his arms, holding her close.

"He died, Josiah. Champ died." The words came out in a whisper.

"Sweetheart, I'm so sorry." He took the phone, thanked the vet and then held her while she sobbed out her grief. "Let me take you home. I'll come back and take care of this later."

Leah sniffed. "I need my car to get to work tomorrow."

"Okay. I'll drive you and have a friend pick me up."

"You don't have to."

"Yes, I do. You're in no shape to drive yourself." He guided her down the stairs.

"I'd really like to go by Mom and Dad's to check on Lady. I know she's missing Champ."

Josiah thought about returning to the house where he'd

embarrassed himself. He needed to do this for Leah. "Sure. We can do that."

Tears tracked down her face and Josiah pulled a tissue from a box sitting on the counter. "You okay?"

Afraid anything more would set her off again, Leah managed a nod. "I have to tell Mom and Dad."

"Not tonight. You can get yourself together and tell them tomorrow."

"But... Kevin has to know what to do with Champ's bodddyyy." The word stretched out in a wail and his arm went about her shoulder.

"I'm sure the vet can keep him for another day or so. Where's your purse?"

"In the car."

"Your keys?"

"On the hall entry table. Your mom suggested I keep them there so they didn't accidentally get caught up in the sorting upstairs."

He grabbed her hand and pulled her toward the front door. There he paused to grab her keys and set the alarm code before he walked her to her car, his arm about her shoulders. He helped her inside and then went around to the driver's seat.

"You remember where my parents live?"

He remembered it well. Their address was branded into his brain.

They traveled in silence. Leah thought Josiah must not know what to say or do. He parked in the driveway and she met him at the front of the car. She took the keys, unlocked the door and punched in a code before turning on the lights and going in search of their cat.

Lady slept curled up on an afghan on the family room sofa. Leah picked her up and smoothed her hands over the sleek white fur. Lady's face, ears and tail were dark. She pulled her close to her chest and felt reassured by the Siamese's rumbling purr. Leah sank down on the sofa, keeping Lady close and the tears sprang to her eyes again. "I'm useless. Mom and Dad ask so little of me. I always let them down."

Sobs racked her body as Leah gave in to the emotions that swamped her.

Josiah sat next to her and placed an arm around her shoulder. "Shhh. Leah. Stop. Don't blame yourself. You said Champ was elderly. When our time comes, we die. It can't be stopped."

He grabbed tissues from the box on the end table and tenderly dried her face.

Why couldn't she explain? It was more than losing Champ.

Leah sniffed. "I have to call them."

Josiah shook his head and held on to her when she would have stood. "Not tonight. It's late and you're emotional. Get some rest and do it tomorrow when you're thinking more clearly."

She managed a sad smile. "Thanks, Josiah."

"Once you find out what they want to do, I'll help you carry out their plans."

"I can handle it." Not if the sound of her voice was anything to go by, she thought.

"I want to help. It's a tough time and I'd like to provide a shoulder to lean on."

She'd always had someone to lean on during bad times. Could Josiah say the same? She knew Cecily had been there for him when he was hurting. "Thanks."

They sat together for a few minutes longer. "Are you going to spend the night here?"

She shook her head. "I need to go home. I'll come by early in the morning to check on Lady."

"Come on. I'll drive you and call my buddy to pick me up at your place."

She keyed in the alarm and they locked up the house,

leaving Lady asleep on the afghan. She'd miss Champ more tomorrow when she couldn't find him. They would all miss Champ.

She gave Josiah the address for her condo and he drove them over.

Leah stood on the sidewalk. "Come inside while you wait."

"Thanks, but I'll wait here. He's not that far away."

Leah nodded. "Thanks for everything, Josiah."

"You're welcome."

She walked to the entrance of her building and turned back to wave goodbye.

"Leah, wait."

He ran over to where she stood.

"Is it okay if I call you tomorrow? Just to see how you're doing?"

Her purse slipped down her arm and Leah jerked it up onto her shoulder. "You don't have to…"

"I want to."

She nodded. "I'd like that."

"Good. I'll talk to you in the morning."

His friend drove up. Josiah said good-night and walked toward the truck.

She smiled and lifted her hand in farewell when he turned to wave one last time.

Chapter 7

"I'm so sorry about your dog. Is there anything I can do?"

Leah smiled at Cecily. Her head ached from crying so much the night before and that morning her eyes were so red and swollen that there were no eye drops on the market strong enough to help them. She appreciated the Byrds' offers of assistance during this time when she missed her parents the most.

Josiah had called early that morning. He'd asked how she felt and then surprised her by asking if she'd go out with him Friday night. She'd debated whether she should say yes. She didn't know if he was being a nice guy and trying to take her mind off what had happened or was being honest when he said he wanted to spend time with her. She'd said yes. When she asked what she should wear, he suggested they keep this one casual. His implication there would be more dates, possibly more formal, pleased Leah.

"Josiah offered to help. I took the coward's way out and

emailed my parents early this morning. They're on their way to London so I don't know when I'll hear back."

"Time-wise they're ahead of us so I imagine you'll hear soon."

Leah hated sharing the news, particularly during their time of celebration. "Ready to tackle that hall closet?"

Cecily started up the stairs. "Josiah took the trash down for us last night. I'm thinking we should use smaller bags. I can understand why people get those construction Dumpsters."

Leah chuckled. "Not for organizing their home."

"It could work. We could toss stuff out the window."

"Maybe for the attic, if you plan to toss everything. There's probably an ordinance prohibiting Dumpsters in this area."

They quickly sorted through the odds and ends left over from the previous day. Photos and a few of the decorative pieces went into the keep pile and others were wrapped and placed in boxes to be donated. They worked well together. Cecily pulled out items and told Leah where they needed to go. Only when she tottered on the fence did Leah make a suggestion.

Cecily wasn't about to part with old children's board games held together with yellowed tape and boxes of music on cassette tapes and old albums.

Leah stood, her hands filled with the plastic cassette cases. "Do you have a player for these?"

Cecily nodded. "Our system plays both. And I have a unit that converts them to CDs."

"But do you have time to do that?"

"It's on my list."

"Okay, though most of the songs probably aren't favorites. You could just as easily download those you like on your iPhone and enjoy them now, without the extra work."

Leah slipped the cassettes into the keep/think about bin and hoped Cecily would rethink her stance on the outdated items. Nostalgia was fine on the walls of restaurants but use-less when it came to well-organized homes.

They carried the smaller bags of garbage downstairs when they stopped for lunch. As always, the kitchen took Leah's breath away. The custom-made cabinets in a dark wood and quartz countertops in a light color were glorious. Her mother would love this room. Renovating the kitchen had always been on her parents' "one day" list. Leah had wondered why they didn't buy a newer home but knew they felt a strong emotional attachment to the home they had lived in since moving back to Wilmington.

Cecily moved over to the sink to wash her hands before going to the fridge.

"I'll have Josiah move those donate boxes to the garage. That will give us more room to work and make things easier when it comes to taking them away."

"If we made lists of the contents, I could take them by the donation site. Just to keep the numbers down."

Cecily eyed Leah. "And to keep me from changing my mind?"

Leah placed her hands on her hips and looked the woman in the eye. "That's what Josiah said last night. Have you been going through the boxes after I leave?"

Cecily chortled. "No. I'm positive about the items in the donate boxes. Can't say the same about this keep/rethink pile you have me using."

Leah repeated the phrase she'd been hoping to imprint on Cecily. "Just remember, items you can't find when you want or need them are basically useless."

"And how many times do I have to tell myself that before it sinks in?"

"I've been thinking and if you really have to keep some-thing the key is making sure you can find it when you want it. We can make lists and post them in the closet or get a notebook and log where you store things. Whichever you think is best."

Cecily eyed her suspiciously. "Who are you and what have you done with Leah?"

They laughed together.

"You really do need to prioritize the keep/think about items."

"I know I'm being silly about this."

Leah shook her head. "No, you're not. Too many people have to condense a lifetime of treasures to fit into new living accommodations. Just remember that Josiah may not feel the same connection to certain items that you do so keep what's most important to you. If there are things you feel he would want, you could make a list and talk to him about them."

"That's a wonderful idea."

Cecily removed croissants from the toaster oven and sliced them in half, adding homemade chicken salad. She spooned cucumber, corn and tomato summer salad onto the plates and handed one to Leah.

They sat at the kitchen island. Leah said grace and took a bite of the sandwich. "This is delicious. You're such a good cook."

"Thank you. It's nice to have someone to appreciate my efforts. Do you cook?"

"Not much. Mom taught me a few basics but I hate cooking for one."

Cecily nodded. "I had plenty of time and opportunity to cook. Even Jim, Joseph's father, couldn't complain. And believe me he was a critical man."

Leah couldn't begin to imagine what it would be like to live with someone who never had a positive comment.

"At first, I wanted to move out but Joseph said we didn't have anywhere to go and he wasn't about to start work before he finished school. He was certain that once his dad sank his claws into him he'd never escape."

"Was it so bad?"

Cecily considered that. "Joseph and his father would argue for hours on end. Sometimes I think Jim gave in to shut him up."

"What about Josiah? Did he argue with his dad?"

"Not so much. He internalized his frustrations."

"Not good."

"I would encourage him to tell his father what he thought but he believed Joseph didn't care. I'm not sure I didn't do Josiah a disservice by not encouraging him to find work elsewhere."

"Why do you suppose he worked with his dad?"

"I don't think he ever gave up hope of having a relationship with his father. Maybe he thought they could bond through work."

After they finished their sandwiches and salad, Cecily picked up a knife and sliced into a strawberry-rhubarb pie. "Hope you like this. It's my favorite and I've been hoping for an excuse to have one."

Leah savored the first bite of pie. "Feel free to use me as an excuse any time."

As they chatted, Leah debated mentioning their upcoming date. She concluded that if Josiah wanted his mother to know he would tell her.

After lunch, they finished the hall closet and moved to another closet. Leah's phone rang and she excused herself upon seeing her father's number on the screen.

"Leah, sweetie, we just got your message. I'm so sorry about Champ."

The sound of her mother's voice made Leah tear up again. "He wouldn't eat or move or anything."

"Poor baby," Marty cooed. "I wish we were there. Don't be sad, sweetie. Champ lived a long, happy life."

"I know but he…" *I can handle this,* she told herself. "Tell me what you want to do and I'll call Kevin."

"You don't need to do anything. Daddy and I have decided to have Champ cremated and sprinkle his ashes under those shade trees in the backyard he loved so much. Daddy has already sent Kevin an email. We'll have a little memorial service when we get home."

Relief that the burden had been lifted off her filled Leah and then guilt for being so useless. Her parents deserved better. "I checked on Lady last night and again this morning. She's her usual independent self. I can't tell if she misses Champ."

"She'll be fine."

Leah hoped so. She couldn't stand the thought of losing another pet. She changed the subject. "How's London?"

"Wonderful. Your dad booked a hop on, hop off tour on an open-topped double-decker bus for tomorrow. We'll see Buckingham Palace and so many other places. There's a ninety-minute walking tour of the Changing of the Guard and a Thames River Cruise. There's so much to see and do. We miss you, though. You have to come with us next time."

Leah wondered when that would be. Her mother wasn't home from this trip and was already making plans for the future. "I'll let you go. You have sightseeing to do. Give Daddy my love."

"Don't hang up. He's right here and wants to talk to you."

Leah listened to her father's reassurances before ending the call. God had truly blessed her with wonderful parents. Even when she'd offered to call Kevin again, her father said no.

"Your parents?" Cecily asked when Leah returned.

She nodded. "Daddy's already handled the arrangements. He wouldn't hear of me doing anything. He's very protective of Mom and me."

"Men often feel that way regarding the women in their lives."

"I know, but I'd like to do things for them some time. All I do is take, take, take."

"Nothing they don't freely give."

Leah knew Cecily understood the situation from a parent's point of view but didn't feel any better.

They had church that evening and agreed to an early wrap-up. Leah stopped to pick up cat food and felt sad as she passed the display of dog play toys Champ loved so much. It had always been nearly impossible to walk out without buying one for him. She drove over to her parents' and found Lady under their bed.

Leah lay down on her stomach and coaxed the cat out. She rolled over and sat up, cuddling Lady to her chest. "Hey, girl, are you lonely?" The Siamese rumbled and purred beneath her hands.

"Guess what, Lady? That guy, Josiah, who came over with me last night. He asked me out and I said yes. He's a really nice person."

They sat together for a while before she stood and went to take care of the litter box. Afterward, she filled Lady's water and food bowls.

The sight of Champ's empty bowls and leash drove her to the garage in search of a box. Leah cleaned his bowls and packed them away. Then she moved through the house in search of his other items and cried at the sight of a well-used chew toy. She couldn't help but remember when he was a puppy and her mother despaired of him chewing up everything in their house.

Leah sniffed and dumped the toy in the trash, doubting

her mom would want to hold on to it for even the most senti-
mental of reasons. She carried the box and Champ's bed into
the garage. After securing and marking the box, she placed
it out of sight on the back garage shelving unit.

Back inside, she washed up in the half bath and grabbed
a bottle of water from the fridge. She paused to give Lady
one last pat before heading home.

The mailbox caught her eye on the way out and she stopped
to remove the day's mail. She'd been so intent on checking
on Lady that she'd forgotten. No packages today. She went
back inside and glanced through the pile before laying it on
her mother's desktop.

In an almost natural progression, her thoughts shifted from
the mail to Josiah. She wondered what he was doing right
now. Was he out with a client? Or thinking how stupid he'd
been for asking her out? Maybe even regretting his rash action? She hoped not. Leah liked Josiah. As she'd told Lady,
he was a nice guy.

It had been a while since her last date and though she
had no idea what he planned, she looked forward to Friday
night. Most often her dates were dinner and a movie or sitting around on someone's patio or in their living room listening to her date talk with his friends and feeling left out.

Knowing Josiah and Cecily made this date seem more
personal. She had bonded with the Byrds and wanted to hear
Josiah tell her about himself. She wanted to know him and
even the thought of meeting his friends seemed an exciting
prospect.

Last night, before she'd cried herself to sleep, her grief
over Champ turned to her own inadequacies and her growing
frustrations at where her life was headed. At a loss to understand this sudden need to accomplish something major with
her life, Leah prayed and asked God to bless her, to guide her

along the path He had for her and to give her the desires of her heart. She wanted to be loved and give love. Those were her most urgent needs.

That night she sat in the sanctuary with her friends and listened to Pastor Paul's midweek message. She'd been surprised when the church officials chose this young man to lead their church, but after hearing him preach she knew why. Every message seemed as if God intended them for her. Tonight's topic was "turmoil" and she could definitely relate.

As they walked out to their cars, Leah glanced at her friend. "What was that scripture Pastor Paul used tonight?"

Susan pulled the note she'd written from her Bible. "Job 3:25 and 26. 'I have no peace, no quietness; I have no rest, but only turmoil.'"

Leah had known Susan all her life. They had been in the same Sunday school classes growing up, attended the same school and then after graduation Susan chose to get married while Leah went to college.

"You ever feel like that?"

"Who hasn't?"

Leah nodded. "Thank God I don't have Job's problems, but I have the turmoil. You want to go for ice cream and talk more?"

Susan said yes. "Let me tell Eddie and you can drop me off at home later."

They climbed into Leah's SUV. "Fast food cone or Dairy Queen?"

"Let's splurge. I haven't been to the Dairy Queen in forever."

The small building that housed the ice cream shop was surrounded by cars. Leah found a place to park and they took their place in line, waiting to give their order. A few minutes later, they took their cups of ice cream with extras and returned to the car where they sat eating and talking.

Voices and a hint of a breeze floated in through the open car window. It was a humid, late June evening and Leah knew the flashes of lightning in the distance meant a storm before morning.

"I have a date Friday night."

Susan's spoon paused in midair. "Really? With who? What does he do? Where did you meet him?"

"Whoa, girl. Josiah Byrd. He's in commercial real estate." Leah considered Josiah's need for secrecy before answering the last question. "He stopped by Mom and Dad's a couple of weeks ago. I gave him my business card and his mom hired me."

"Sweeeet." Susan's extended version of the word made Leah laugh. "Work and a man, too. Great combination. Where's he taking you?"

"I don't know. He's making the plans. I'm looking forward to our date. He's a nice guy and not bad on the eyes, either."

"Maybe he's the one. I'm praying for you. Sorry about Champ. You should have called me."

"Josiah drove me home. We were having dinner at his mom's house."

Susan frowned. "I thought this was your first date?"

"It is. He surprised his mom with takeout and she had other plans so he invited me to eat with him. Then the vet called and I got upset and he wouldn't let me drive myself home."

"Sounds like a keeper."

Leah spooned ice cream into her mouth. After swallowing, she plunged off the deep end. "He called to check on me the next morning and asked me out. You don't think it's a pity date, do you?"

"Don't be silly. The guy likes what he sees."

She ate another bite and groaned when the cold headache struck.

"Touch your tongue to the roof of your mouth."

Once she was back in control, Leah said, "You're so good for my self-esteem. Susan, will you pray for me?"

"You know I will. Tell me what's wrong?"

Leah heard the concern in Susan's voice. "I'm feeling so frustrated about where I am in life."

Her friend lifted one shoulder. "Depression over our life path isn't abnormal."

"Yeah, but I'm feeling pretty defeated right now."

"Why? You're working and you have a date."

"I haven't accomplished much with my life. I spoke with Mom and Dad today. They're so in love and having the time of their lives. I hated having to tell them about Champ."

"Is it grief, Leah? I mean… Well, Champ's been around for a long time."

She dropped the spoon back in the container. "That might be some of it but I've had this feeling for a while now. I can't help but think about where I should be at my age. Most women at least have a significant other if they aren't married. Some are even working on second husbands."

Susan looked surprised. "I'm sure that's not what you want."

Leah shook her head. "No way. I want one man who loves me in the same way I love him. One who believes in lifetime commitment."

"Sounds like you're having an early crisis. Lots of people hit a wall around thirty. It's been on my mind too. You know how much Eddie and I want a baby. Think it over. You know what you want. What's stopping you from having it?"

"It's more than that, Susan. Sometimes I feel my life has been too easy. I've been blessed with wonderful parents, a beautiful home and good education and here I am struggling to keep a floundering business going and not using the education my parents paid for."

"Is business that bad?"

Leah shrugged. "God provides. Every time I'm sure it's my last job, something comes through. But I'm tired of living on the edge. I want security. I don't want to be that adult child who goes running home to her parents when her life falls apart."

"How long have you been doing this now?"

"Three years. And I still work part-time at the clinic to supplement my income."

"Are you trying to find yourself?"

Leah hooted. "No. I consider myself pretty much found but I do feel I'm in limbo."

"Have you written down your plans? I read that people who do that are often successful."

"That's a thought."

"I think you're beating yourself up for no reason. The economy is pretty tough right now. Just having enough work to pay expenses is good."

"That's all I'm doing. No savings. No retirement. If something happens, I'd have to ask my parents for help. Sad for someone my age, don't you think?"

"Be thankful you have parents who can help you. Eddie and I are scraping along, living from check to check. Every time we get a little bit ahead, the car tears up or something happens to the house. I think it's a conspiracy. Our possessions check our bank balance or something."

Leah chuckled. "The missing socks and clothes hangers probably tell them." Thankfully her car was newer and the condo hadn't required a great deal of repair.

"You asked for prayer, but I'll give you my opinion first. If you aren't happy with your life as it is, change it. You're the only one who can. Think about what you really want and go after your goals. Same thing with being in love—find someone and make it happen."

"It's not that easy."

"It is when you meet the right person. You know when the guy is right for you. I felt that way with Eddie."

Leah thought about her mother. Evidently her father hadn't been her first choice if she'd thought she would marry Joseph Byrd. Had she known Joseph was the one?

"You're right. If I want change, I have to adjust my way of thinking. I can't go through life hanging on to the idea that one day Mr. Right will drop into my lap and I'll become a stay-at-home wife and mother."

"Is that what you want?"

"I think so. But I'm so confused."

"Let's pray for clarity." Susan reached over and took Leah's hand and sent up a prayer that Leah would have a clear mind as she planned for her future and that God would send the man He intended into her life.

"You're a smart woman."

Susan grinned. "Yeah, attribute it to my school of hard knocks degree. You'd better take me home. I told Eddie I'd be there in an hour or so."

Leah hopped out and tossed their trash and then drove her friend home. She parked in front of Susan's house. "See you Sunday. Thanks for the advice."

"Thanks for the ice cream. And stop worrying. Life has a way of dropping wonderful things on us when we least expect it."

Chapter 8

Since Josiah hadn't told her where they were going, Leah dressed in a knee-length jean skirt, a royal blue sleeveless top and sandals. She pulled her hair back and clipped it at the base of her neck. It had been hot when she arrived home an hour earlier and thanks to a sudden heat wave it didn't appear the evening would be much cooler.

When she opened the door to Josiah, he wore khaki shorts with a green golf shirt with a Byrd company logo and Top-Siders. Leah had never seen him dressed this casually. "Come in. You look comfortable."

"Better than those stuffed turkey images?"

Leah blushed. "You aren't going to forget that, are you?"

He pretended hurt. "You laughed at me."

"Not at you. I couldn't help the image that floated through my head with that comment."

"Okay, you're forgiven." He glanced around her condo. "Nice place. I like the brick walls. They give the place character."

Those walls and the high ceilings had convinced Leah to buy the condo. It was located in a renovated historic downtown building. The spacious floor plan offered plenty of storage and an updated kitchen with new appliances and granite. Her parents had liked the security entrance. Leah loved that she could walk to a number of shops and restaurants downtown whenever she wanted.

"I'd give you a tour but you've pretty much seen all there is except for the bathroom and bedroom."

"I'm impressed. My condo is rather plain compared to yours."

Leah doubted that. His taste was too good to ever live in a bland condo. And his mother surely wouldn't allow him to live in a dump. "I'm sure it's beautiful. Cecily said you'd taken pieces from the house. She has beautiful taste."

With her comment, Josiah backpedaled. "On second thought, don't tell my mom I said that. She decorated the place and while it's not exactly my taste, she did a great job."

She met his smile with one of her own. Leah pretended to zip her lip. "We'll just keep that our little secret."

"Thanks. I thought we'd have dinner at the LongHorn Steakhouse and then check out the *Music on the Town* concert on the Mayfaire event field. It starts at six but I thought we would let it cool down a bit first."

His plans impressed Leah. She hated those dates where they volleyed back and forth over what to do. "Sounds good. Would you like something to drink before we go?"

"I'll wait until we get to the restaurant."

He escorted her out to a black Mercedes very like the one his mother drove, his hand hovering near her lower back. "Where's the truck?"

"At home. This was Dad's car. Mom keeps saying I should keep something of his but I already had this. I'm using it as a company car."

Josiah opened the door and Leah slipped inside. She ran a hand over the beautiful leather upholstery, admiring his luxury ride. A definite step up from her small SUV. He went around and climbed in behind the wheel. He glanced at her. "You and Mom have a good day?"

"Emotional. She got into another box of memorabilia that left her teary-eyed."

He scowled. "I hate this. She's making herself miserable."

Leah recognized the same protective tendencies in Josiah that she saw in her father. "She tells me they're happy tears. Actually, reminiscing might help with her grief. She was excited about our date."

He pulled up to the stop sign and waited for oncoming traffic before turning. Josiah glanced at her. "Do you mind that I told her?"

Leah shook her head. "I started to mention it but then questioned whether you'd want her to know."

"I don't keep a lot of secrets from Mom. I asked if she wanted to come along when I borrowed the lawn chairs."

Her heart plummeted to her stomach. So much for any hopes that something wonderful might be in the offing.

"That would have been fine. I like Cecily."

He chuckled. "I know you do. She likes you, too. But there's no way she would intrude on my love life. Particularly when she likes the girl involved."

Love life? Leah felt her skin redden a little. She'd been hopeful but had not advanced to thoughts of a love life just yet.

"Everything okay with Champ's arrangements?"

A fresh surge of sadness and despair washed over her. "Daddy sent an email to the vet. I feel bad that he had to handle it while on vacation."

"You shouldn't. I'm sure he felt it was his responsibility."

He turned off Market onto Eastwood Road. "So, Leah Wright, tell me something about you I don't know."

She reclined into the comfortable leather seat. "You pretty much know everything there is to know."

He looked doubtful. "What's your favorite color?"

Certain he expected her to name some girly color, Leah said, "Depends on my mood. I'm a chameleon."

"A chameleon, huh?" He grinned. "Hate to tell you but that blue is too pretty for you to blend into the scenery."

"Just wait."

He laughed heartily. "Not even you can pull that one off. So you have lots of favorite colors?"

She turned toward him in her seat. "I do. What about you?"

"Blue is good. Lighter shades, like the Carolina blue sky."

"That's the Tarheel in you coming out. Why do so many men like blue?"

"You mean like little girls and pink? It is our birth indicator color. Maybe we think it's easier to hang on to the idea for life once it's introduced to us."

Leah found herself entranced by his low-pitched voice. "That's the problem with learning your baby's sex in advance. No sunny yellow or pastel green nurseries. Would you have a different favorite color if you'd been introduced to other colors?"

"I doubt Mom knew whether she was having a boy or girl," he said. "You wouldn't want to know the sex of your baby?"

"It's very practical," she began. "But I like the idea of a surprise."

He nodded. "Me, too."

"I know my mom would probably have to know. She's very into details when it comes to entertaining. She loves those baby announcement parties where they slice the cake to show the sex of the baby."

Thinking it was too early in their relationship for so much

information on babies, Leah asked him another question and by the time Josiah parked at the restaurant they knew each other's birth dates, the last books they'd read and where they went to church.

He escorted her into the Western-themed restaurant where they found they had beaten the Friday-night crowd. Probably the place would be filled by the time they finished their meal. They were escorted to a booth and left with their menus.

They soon had their drink orders placed and a loaf of warm bread. Josiah offered her the basket and then pulled off a slice for himself. He spread butter lavishly and took a bite.

"I'm hungry. I skipped lunch. Hope you like steak?" He frowned. "I suppose I should have asked before choosing this place."

"There's not much I won't eat. Mom's rule was that we ate what she put on the table or did without so I have fairly diverse tastes." Then she qualified, "Except for the things I vowed I wouldn't eat once I became an adult."

Josiah grinned at that. "Me, too. Know what you want?"

"The grilled chicken and strawberry salad and a sweet potato with cinnamon butter and sugar."

"Sounds good."

She glanced down at the menu and then back at him. "Josiah, I wanted to thank you for being so helpful the other night and to apologize for that pity party I forced on you."

"Don't be so hard on yourself. You experienced a tragic loss."

"It's more than that. Oh, never mind. I'm just dealing with my insecurities."

"About what?"

She sounded like a real loser. If she told him the truth he'd never ask her out again. Everyone murmured platitudes to make her feel better about herself every time she brought up the subject. "Where I am in life. Oh, never mind. That conversation is too heavy for a first date."

He laid down the menu and paid closer attention to what she said. "I'm a good listener if you need to talk."

Leah touched his hand and was surprised when he flipped it palm up and closed his fingers about hers.

"You are a good listener but I think we need lighter conversation."

He nodded. "So what do you do for fun?"

That was too easy. "I love to read, and I often hang out with my church friends. I see them two or three times a week. I sing in the choir. And volunteer when we have church work days. And I've been painting my condo."

"You stay busy."

"My organized home gives me more free time." Leah grinned at him.

"What about your college friends?"

"Things aren't the same. Everyone has their own life and our paths rarely cross. Some are off pursuing careers. Others are married and having kids."

"Same here. I get tired of being the odd man out."

Leah knew exactly how he felt. "They invite you out of a sense of obligation but hope you have other plans or at least find a date."

"Yeah, they feel guilty because you're all alone and think it's their duty to entertain this single guest who can't seem to find someone to love."

Leah smiled and pointed at him. "Do you know my friends?"

He chuckled and said, "Maybe their doppelgängers."

A sudden revelation hit her. "Josiah, this is what your mom is experiencing with her friends. They must feel uncomfortable because she lost her husband. Maybe even guilty because they're thankful it wasn't them."

Josiah raised his brows and nodded. "Good point. I'll have to mention that to her."

"Okay, next question. What's your favorite dessert?" Leah was a dessert fiend. She loved ice cream most of all.

"Birthday cake. I like the frosting."

Leah smiled and pulled a hand up to touch her chest. "Me, too. I never turn down birthday cake."

"Want me to tell them it's your birthday?"

She gasped and laughed at the same time. "No."

"Okay, should I tell them it's mine?"

She shook her head at his playfulness. "They don't bring birthday cake."

He looked little boy disappointed. "Then we'll both order the best dessert on the menu and celebrate our birthdays."

The waitress appeared at that moment and looked from one to the other. "It's your birthdays?"

"No." Leah and Josiah responded in unison.

The young woman looked confused.

"First date," Josiah said as to explain their conversation.

"Oh." She didn't look convinced. "Ready to order? Or do you need more time?"

They told her what they wanted and watched the woman walk away before breaking into laughter.

"Well, it's official. She thinks we're nuts."

"She shouldn't judge us on hearing only part of the conversation."

Leah sorted out her silverware. "So how's the real estate world? Make any big deals this week?"

"A couple of leases. Lots of people looking, few buying."

"Their dreams don't match their wallets?"

"Something like that. Or else reality strikes cold dead fear in their hearts. Where are your parents this week?"

"London. They move on to Ireland next week and then home."

"Spain, Paris, London and Ireland. That's quite a trip."

"Dad picked the top four places Mom always wanted to visit. She's loving every minute of it. This trip will be her all-time favorite gift."

"Quite a gift." His expression grew serious. "You know Mom is going to want to see your dad when they get back."

Leah nodded. "And you're concerned."

"I am. Mom has no idea why our fathers stopped being friends. She's sure to ask how long your dad has been back in Wilmington and why he didn't look them up."

She could feel him bouncing his knee underneath the table. He was nervous, and rightfully so. "We can't control this, Josiah. I'm sure my parents won't freely offer an explanation of what transpired with your father."

"I hope not."

She touched his hand. "Give it to God. Trust Him to take care of your mom."

Their food arrived and the conversation ceased with the consumption of food. "How's your sweet potato?"

"Delicious." Leah scooped up a bite. "Want to taste?"

He did. "It's good." He cut off a piece of steak and returned the favor.

"Um, good." Leah enjoyed the tender bite of steak.

A few minutes later she patted her stomach and declared, "I couldn't eat another bite."

"No dessert?" He looked disappointed.

"Maybe later."

Josiah paid the check and took her hand as they walked out to the car.

"Thanks for dinner."

"Thanks for the company."

They drove over to the concert area and found a parking space. He pulled two chairs from the trunk and carried them over to where people sat on blankets and in chairs watching the band perform. Children ran about the area, their voices rising in the warm summer evening as they played in bounce houses. He rested one chair against his leg and opened the other, indicating she should have a seat. Then he opened his own and sat down. The band performed a mixture of country and pop music.

Her gaze shifted over the area. "This is nice."

The band finished another song and they applauded. "I read about the concerts but this is a first for me. Mostly I do dinner and a movie or hang out with friends watching sports."

"Crowds aren't generally my thing." Leah felt she had admitted something major to him. "I prefer small gatherings with family and friends."

"Good to know."

"What about you? What do you like?"

"I'm more of a small-group person."

Leah smiled at him. "So we've both stepped outside our comfort zones and found it's not too bad after all?"

"Looks that way."

She tapped her foot to the music as the band continued to perform. When they took a short break, they sat waiting for breezes in the unseasonably warm June night. Leah swiped at her forehead, feeling the perspiration and wondering what it was doing to her makeup. She should have known better. She fanned her face with her hand, shooing away the gnats. "It's so humid."

"I should have bought insect repellent. It never did cool down like I thought it might. Had enough?" At her nod, Josiah said, "Let's go."

She folded her chair and held it under her arm. Josiah held out a hand. "Let me take that."

"I've got it."

At the car, he removed a boogie board to get the chairs back inside the trunk. "You any good with that?" Leah asked.

"Pretty good."

"You a surfer dude?"

"Not so much."

He opened her door. "What do you think? Should we visit an ice cream shop?"

Leah grinned at him. "Your sweet tooth begging for satisfaction?"

"Good way to cool off."

"Or we could pick up a fast food dip-cone and go for a walk on the beach."

"Yeah. I like that idea even better."

They bought ice cream cones and drove down to Wrightsville Beach. Josiah parked in the public access next to the big hotel on Lumina Avenue. Both left their shoes behind and climbed over the hills of sand leading to the ocean. It was low tide. They walked across damp sand, leaving a trail of footprints behind them. The incoming waves felt wonderful against their bare feet and legs.

The wind whipped tendrils of hair loose from the clasp. Leah shoved them back and licked the cone several times, hoping to keep the melting ice cream from running over her fingers.

"Maybe this wasn't such a good idea," she said.

"There's a trash barrel. Want to dump them?"

"No. It may be messy but it's good ice cream." The vanilla soft serve was very creamy and twisted upwards on the cone. "Eat faster."

They raced to finish and laughed when it was a tie, each crunching the last bite of their cones at the same time.

Josiah rinsed his hand in the ocean, slinging off the excess water. "Let's walk that off."

Leah stuck the paper band from the cone in her pocket and rinsed her hands, rubbing them dry. They walked toward the pier in the distance, light coming from the half-moon and structures on the shore.

"This breeze feels wonderful." She picked up her pace, trying to keep up with his longer steps.

"Why didn't you tell me to slow down?" Josiah stopped and took her hand in his. "I'm sorry. It's not a race."

They walked a bit farther before he suggested they turn back. The heat made her tired and Leah was more than ready to head for home. At the car, Josiah took a towel from the trunk and brushed the sand off her feet.

She looked down at him as he knelt before her. "Thank you, kind sir."

He grinned, stood up and leaned in to press a gentle kiss on her lips. "Nothing's too good for you, my lady."

Chapter 9

Watching the incoming passengers, Leah spotted her parents and waved at them from the area in front of the baggage claim.

They beamed when they caught sight of her. Leah hurried forward and was wrapped in a three-way hug. "Welcome home. It's so good to have you back. I've missed you."

Marty took Leah's face in her hands and kissed her cheek. "We missed you, too."

Ben slipped an arm about her waist and hugged her again. "It's good to be home."

"How was Ireland? And your flight?"

"Beautiful. Long."

Leah laughed. "I imagine even your jet lag is confused with all the moving around you've been doing."

The buzzer sounded and the carousel began to move. Ben took a step forward and said, "I'll get our luggage."

Marty grasped Leah's hand in hers. "We need to help. I had to buy an extra suitcase to bring home all our goodies."

More stuff, Leah thought as she walked with her mother.

"We took lots of pictures. And Ben shot lots of video. Just wait until you see how incredible these places are."

Her mother's enjoyment of their travels thrilled Leah. She deserved every moment. She'd done the kid-friendly vacations for many years so this had been even more special for her. No doubt she looked forward to sharing her experience with everyone. Leah knew with certainty that there would be photos in the Wright family newsletter this Christmas.

Soon they were loaded in the SUV and headed for home. Leah had stocked their fridge the previous day and checked to make sure the house was ready for their arrival. Before leaving for the airport she'd put a pork loin in the slow cooker and placed fresh flowers on the entry hall table to welcome them.

Her father parked in the driveway and they carried the bags upstairs. They left her mother in the bedroom and went downstairs to the family room. Ben flopped down on the sofa and inhaled. "Smells good."

"I thought you might be hungry. I've got potato salad, corn and fresh tomatoes from the farmers' market. And I made a pitcher of tea."

He grinned. "Now I know I'm home."

"You want a glass now?"

He nodded and Leah went off to prepare iced tea for everyone. She returned to the living room and handed him a glass. She placed her mother's on a coaster on the end table and went back to get her own. Leah sat in the armchair, lifting her legs up onto the footstool. "So did you enjoy yourself?"

He nodded. "I really did. I wasn't so sure when I first contacted that travel agent but after seeing the joy on your mom's face these past weeks, I'm glad we did this. I think I made up for all those bad gifts."

"You did. Would you go again?"

He nodded thoughtfully. "I would. In fact, I plan to take your mother on more trips in the future. Shorter trips, mind you. Though she was talking about Alaska and Australia on the way home. I hope she doesn't plan to run the alphabet."

Leah laughed. "Good thing we mailed out that flyer last week. You're going to need more patients if she does."

"How did that go?"

"Great. I delivered it to the printer and they handled the mailing. I suppose we'll know soon enough if it's successful. We included the whitening coupon you suggested."

He nodded. "So what have you been up to while we were away?"

Though they had communicated regularly there were little details that were missed. "Mom told you about her letter?"

He nodded, his brown eyes searching her face. "What on earth possessed you to mail that old letter?"

Her hands shot up. "Stupidity? Though I can say it's brought some new experiences into my life."

"What kind of experiences?"

"Well, I'm working for Cecily Byrd, for one. And I've been on a few dates with Josiah Byrd." They'd been out three more times. He'd suggested a trip to the beach on Sunday afternoon. Cecily had joined them for that and they had gone out the following Friday and Saturday night.

That caught his attention. "Really? What's he like?"

"Nice guy. You'd like him. Cecily says you were Joseph Byrd's best friend in high school. She can't wait to see you again."

Ben glanced up from the stack of mail and frowned.

"You don't want to see her?"

"Not particularly. I never had problems with Cecily. But I do have problems with the questions that will arise as a result of seeing her again. And more importantly, how this is going to affect your mother."

Leah understood his reluctance to renew the old friendship. "I'm afraid she's going to ask why you didn't contact Joseph when you came back to Wilmington."

He leaned forward and jerked the pillow from behind his back. "It would have been uncomfortable for everyone involved. Your mom and I made a joint decision to put him out of our lives."

"Didn't you like him anymore?"

"Can't say I liked the man he became. But I am thankful he moved on and gave me the opportunity to win your mother."

Marty entered the room and sat down next to her husband. "I am not a prize to be won, Ben Wright."

He leaned to kiss her. "So true. You're my gift."

She blushed like a new bride. "Stop it. What were you two talking about?"

"What your daughter's been doing in our absence."

Marty turned to Leah with an enthusiastic smile. "Do tell."

"Well, she's working for Cecily Byrd and dating her son."

Marty looked concerned. "Really? You're dating Josiah Byrd?"

Leah nodded. "He's a nice guy."

"Must not have taken after his father."

The cutting comment was so unlike her mother.

"Josiah isn't his father's biggest fan, either."

"Smart man."

Leah saw her father squeeze her mother's hand. "Mom, I'm sorry. Does it bother you that Josiah and I are dating?"

"Not if you like him. Ironically, this could be God's way of making me forgive Joseph."

That shocked Leah even more. All her life Marty Wright had taught forgive and forget, and here she admitted she hadn't forgiven someone. "I didn't read your letter."

"Thank you for that. I'm mortified that it was read by anyone."

Leah felt lower than dirt. "I'm really sorry, Mom. I told Josiah it was private and he shouldn't have read it in the first place."

"Where is the letter?"

"Josiah has it. Said he was going to destroy it because the contents could devastate his mom. He's very protective of Cecily."

Marty sighed and shook her head in dismay. "I hate this. I never had any intention of telling Cecily Byrd anything about the man she married."

"Would you tell me what happened?"

Marty shook her head. Ben's arm slipped over his wife's shoulder and he pulled her closer. "It's not something I care to discuss."

Leah accepted her mother's stance. "Cecily knows about Dad. She's anxious to see him again."

Marty looked at her husband and rolled her eyes. "And the news just gets better and better."

Leah had never seen this side of her mother. "Cecily's very nice. She hired me to help clear her husband's closet and now we've moved on to the rest of the house."

"And she's won you over because she wants to get organized?"

Leah protested. "No. She really is nice. Like you, she has her moments. Some things I couldn't pry from her fingers. And she says I'll understand better when I'm older and have a family."

"Good for her. You should listen to that advice, particularly during those times you're so devoted to getting rid of people's memories. Just how far did you get here before I stopped you?"

"Mailing the letter was the worst of it. Though I did trash some of your junk mail."

"Not my catalogs, I hope."

"No catalogs."

"Good. Now what's this I smell?"

"Early dinner." Leah stood. "You two rest while I get the food ready to serve."

Marty stood. "I'll help. I've been waited on for a month now. I need to get back to normal."

Mother and daughter worked together dishing up the food and placing it on the kitchen table. Leah refilled their glasses with ice and poured more tea, cutting thin rounds of lemon for everyone.

"Ben, come eat."

They talked and Leah admired the little Eiffel Tower her mother placed on the table.

"There are a few other things in my new suitcase."

"Mom." Leah groaned.

"You can't go on a trip like this and not buy souvenirs."

"Yes, you can. Just say no."

"You say no. I like my little trinkets. Nothing useless," Marty promised.

Leah glanced at the little tower and eyed her mother.

"That's a decorative ornamental piece that will look great in your condo."

"Yeah, all my friends will want to know when I went to France and I can tell them my parents went."

"Your friends already know you didn't go." She looked hurt. "I thought you'd enjoy it."

Leah felt guilty. She couldn't even be an appreciative daughter. "I will. But you've already sent me so much. Your shipping bill must be outrageous."

Her dad spoke up. "Not so much in the big picture. We shipped a lot of stuff home for us, too."

"I know. I brought boxes in every day. Stacked them in your office."

"Not every day," Marty protested.

"Okay, every other day. You have plenty of new things."

"And more on the way. I bought Christmas gifts and I plan to redo our bedroom in a romantic Parisian theme."

"*Ooh là là.* What do you think about that, Daddy?"

"*C'est la vie.*" He brought his wife's hand to his lips. "*Je t'aime. Je t'adore.*"

Leah chuckled at his French. "What did you say?"

"That's life. I love you. I adore you." He grinned.

"Works for me."

"I'll have you know your dad was the one who suggested we redo our bedroom."

"*Oui.* It was I."

Having her parents back felt good. This had been the longest time they'd ever been apart.

"So tell us what else is going on in Wilmington."

Leah fought back the desire to share her feelings of inadequacy. She would not dump that burden on them tonight. "Nothing new. Josiah and I went over to Mayfaire for a concert on our first date. It was nice. You should check out the schedule."

"Maybe after we dig our way back out from this vacation."

"The concerts will be over by then."

Her dad helped himself to another serving of the pork. "It's back to work and the norm."

Marty glanced at her husband. "The Fourth of July is next week. We have the party." She looked at Leah. "You mailed the invitations, right?"

"Yes, ma'am."

"Make a list of what we need and we'll do the shopping this weekend," Ben said.

"I can help. Cecily has leased a condo at Topsail Beach and plans to live there for the next six months. Said her husband hated the beach and she loves it so she wants to live there. With her move, she only wants to work a couple of days each week, so I'm free."

Marty smiled at her. "Thanks, honey. That will be a big help."

"Would you mind if I invited Josiah and Cecily?"

Her parents looked at each other.

Ben spoke up first. "I'm not sure that's such a good idea."

"I'm sure they already have plans with their friends," Marty said.

Her mom's distress worried Leah more than her father's comment. "I don't think so. Josiah asked if I wanted to go downtown and watch the fireworks with him."

Ben glanced at his wife and back to his daughter. "Let us think about it. We'll give you an answer tomorrow."

"Okay." Leah knew better than to pursue the subject. All her life their decisions had been mutual, based on what they considered best for everyone involved. This one would be no different.

They finished the meal and cleaned up the kitchen. Leah left them to get settled in and headed home.

She could still see her mother's expression when she asked about inviting the Byrds to the party. Leah knew her mom didn't want them there. But she wanted her parents to meet Josiah and Cecily. To see they were nothing like they feared. Her mother's last words lingered in her thoughts.

At the door, Marty had kissed her cheek and whispered, "Protect your heart. The apple doesn't fall far from the tree."

What had she meant by that? Did her mom believe Josiah would hurt her? Had her relationship with his father been so bad that she had no hope for the son? Leah knew the potential for mayhem hovered in the future but could only pray things would be okay.

Well, she'd wait for their decision. Somehow she didn't think her dad could avoid Cecily Byrd for long. Now that she knew he was in Wilmington, she was determined to renew their acquaintance.

At home that night, Josiah called Leah. "Hi. Parents get home okay?"

"I picked them up from the airport and had dinner with them tonight. They had the time of their lives."

"That's good. Mom called. She wants us to go with her to see the beach condo tomorrow. You interested?"

"I told Mom I'd help her but I doubt she'll do much. They're jet-lagged. Sure, I'll go."

"Great. I'll pick you up around nine."

"Aren't you working?"

"I will later. It's important that I see this place and assure myself Mom's going to be safe."

They talked for a few minutes longer before Josiah hung up. He'd become comfortable with Leah and it hadn't struck him as strange that he'd thought to invite her along.

Cecily wanted Leah's help in gathering the items she'd need to make her stay at the beach more comfortable. They could inventory the condo tomorrow and work on packing items from the house and buying anything else she might need.

Josiah picked Leah up early the next morning and took her to breakfast before heading for his mom's new home. The condo was about forty miles away, little more than an hour's drive.

After Cecily showed them around, Leah suggested she fix them something to drink and disappeared into the kitchen.

Josiah liked the unit his mom had leased and admired the view from her balcony. "It's nice but why not Wrightsville or Carolina Beach? They're closer to home."

"And more expensive. I can live here for a fraction of the cost and still see the same beach every day. Besides, eventually I plan to travel and don't want all my funds tied up in a condo."

Josiah had to applaud his mother's frugality. Sure, they had the connections to find her something local more in keeping with her budget but she'd made these plans on her own. He respected that this was what she wanted and fought his urge to control her plans.

"A number of people who live here are close to my age and I've already made new friends. My plan is to take the experience as it comes. I might decide I don't like living at the beach and want to go home. Or I might divide my time between the two homes. We need to see where the future leads us both."

He suspected she meant him dating Leah. She was very happy that the two of them were seeing each other. "Don't get ahead of yourself, Mom."

"Leah's a great girl."

Josiah agreed. Leah had lots of great attributes. She was attractive, loyal, kind and thoughtful. She was an undemanding date, not insisting on expensive restaurants and outings but equally pleased with the simple things, such as an ice cream cone and a walk along the beach.

He'd enjoyed their dates. Leah had a way of making the experience fun no matter what they did. Josiah found himself wanting to keep their dates to the two of them even if they were around strangers.

But there was something else that drew him to her. Something he couldn't quite put his finger on just yet.

His heart told Josiah he cared for Leah. His head warned him to take care. He had no idea where this thing with Leah was headed but figured it couldn't hurt to go along for the ride.

Leah carried the tray out and slid it onto the table. "Iced

tea for everyone. I really like this place, Cecily. I think you're going to enjoy living here."

Cecily put an arm around Leah's waist. "I think so, too."

Chapter 10

"Your father and I discussed your request and decided this might be the best solution for everyone involved."

She'd phoned after her mom got off work to hear their decision. Leah almost wished she'd never asked but since Josiah was in her life she felt it important that her parents get to know him. Tradition from the time she started dating had been for them to get to know the young men she dated. And she didn't feel this was any different.

And while she'd hoped Cecily's new home arrangements might sidetrack her from her intention to see Ben Wright again, Leah was glad her parents agreed.

"This way we'll be part of a larger group and less likely to be uncomfortable."

"Mom, if you think…"

"We want to meet Josiah. And we promise not to prejudge him."

"Thank you. He is not his father. In fact, from what I know, Josiah and his father didn't get along."

"How sad. Has he told you why?"

She could hear pots and pans rattling and knew her mom was preparing dinner. "He felt his father resented his presence."

"That's ridiculous. Joseph made his decisions. Not his son."

"Exactly what I told him. He got upset with me."

Concern changed her mother's tone. Fierce lioness protecting her cub. "Upset? What did he say?"

"Something about me upsetting his life."

Marty relaxed. "Oh, I can understand that."

"Mom."

"Well, you did mail that letter."

"So you're okay with me inviting them?" Leah repeated the question, wanting to be one hundred percent positive she hadn't misunderstood.

"We are. Can you go shopping with me tomorrow? I have a list."

"What time?"

They made arrangements to meet around nine. Leah hung up and called Josiah.

"Mom and Dad are having their annual Fourth of July party next week. Would you like to attend? They want to meet you."

He didn't accept immediately. "Do they know who I am?"

"Yes, Josiah. They know. So will you come?"

"Sure. I love a good party."

"I'm going to call Cecily, too. Mom says it's okay to invite her."

"You're inviting my mother?" Josiah sounded suspicious.

"You know she wants to see Daddy and my parents think a party environment will be easier for everyone involved."

"Your mother won't bring up my dad, will she?"

Would he ever stop harping on that? No matter how many times she reassured him, Josiah feared the situation would blow up in their faces. "Your dad is the last thing my mother wants to talk about. She tells me it's in the past and needs to stay there."

"She's got that right."

"See, you already share something in common. I'll call Cecily's cell."

As Leah thought, Cecily Byrd was very eager to see her old high school friend again.

"I can't wait to see Ben. He was the nicest of Joseph's friends."

And despite all that had happened, Leah had no doubt that her parents would treat Cecily and Josiah well.

"Josiah has directions to my parents' place so we'll see you there next week."

Leah spent the next few days helping her mother prepare for the party. Marty had returned to work on Monday and Leah came over in the afternoons. She rooted decorations out of storage and added some new items they had purchased.

Wreaths, flags, bunting and decorative accessories went up inside and outside the Wright home. Cecily had suggested Leah take the week off and she went over on July 3 to finish the last-minute shopping and prepare the food they would serve the next day.

As always they invited church members, neighbors, her mom's coworkers and her father's partner and office staff. Leah also invited a couple of friends along with the Byrds.

That afternoon, her father checked the weather forecast and with the all clear took responsibility for the tables and chairs, arranging them about the garden. Marty trailed after him, shifting the tables this way and that until she was happy.

When she complained about the lack of color in the garden, Leah drove to the store and purchased trays of annuals. They hadn't planted their usual flowers because of the trip. They worked until dark planting them in beds and planters about the yard. Earlier in the week, Leah had filled tiki lanterns with oil and set out citronella candles to repel the mosquitoes that were as unpopular at outdoor events as ants. They even added a couple of pop-up tents in the sunnier sections of the yard.

The day of the party dawned sunny and bright with clear skies. By 10:00 a.m., the tables sported patriotic coverings and flower arrangements with small flags that fluttered in the warm breeze. Ben set up large coolers filled with ice to chill cans of soda and bottles of water. The party would start around three and continue into the evening.

In the kitchen, her mother carved a watermelon and filled it with balls of sweet melon, cantaloupe and honeydew. The previous evening, she had baked a huge flag cake and made cake pops and brownies that could easily be enjoyed by all. A friend had volunteered to bring banana pudding and Leah knew there would be other contributions as well.

Her father fired up the grills, preparing to cook the burgers, sausages and hot dogs that would feed their guests. The previous evening he'd worked on a pot of his famous chili that he planned to serve on the burgers and dogs.

Leah used a mandolin to slice garden fresh tomatoes and cucumbers. She readied ears of corn for the grill and cried as she sliced onions. Her mother prepared baked beans and coleslaw and a mixture of salads. One of the neighbors sent over jars of bread and butter pickles. The island surrounding her father's grill station would be covered with a bounty of summer foods.

Josiah and Cecily arrived around three-fifteen. Leah greeted them warmly and brought them over to introduce them to her parents. "Cecily and Josiah Byrd, these are my parents, Ben and Marty Wright."

Cecily stepped forward and hugged Ben. "I'd know Ben anywhere. You haven't changed a bit."

While Leah considered her father handsome, she seriously doubted he looked like the youth Cecily had known.

Ben smiled at her. "Cecily, it's great seeing you again. How have you been?"

She smiled prettily. "I'm doing well, thank you. I don't know if Leah told you we lost Joseph to cancer last year."

He nodded. "I'm sorry for your loss."

"I can't tell you how thrilled I was to learn Leah is your daughter. She's beautiful."

"We like to think so." He glanced at Marty and smiled. She stepped forward and took his outstretched hand.

"Nice to meet you, Mrs. Byrd. Josiah."

"Oh. Cecily, please." The women shook hands.

Marty turned to Josiah. "Welcome. We've heard only good things about you from Leah."

He stretched out a hand and shook Marty's and then Ben's hand. "My pleasure."

"How many years has it been?" Cecily went off on a trip down memory lane and Ben flipped burgers and listened as she brought up stories from a time long since forgotten.

Leah could tell her mother didn't like hearing them rehash the past. "We're so glad you could make it today," Marty said to Josiah.

He glanced around at the number of people filling the area. "You throw quite a party."

"Our one summer fling."

"Well, you certainly do it with style."

"Harder this year with us returning from the trip so close to the party but we wouldn't want to miss having everyone over to celebrate. Leah, why don't you get Cecily and Josiah something to drink and introduce them around while I help your father with the grill. We need to get food on the table before we have an uprising on our hands."

Ben smiled. "I'll catch up with you later, Cecily."

An older, tall, rangy man walked up and clapped him on the shoulder. "Need help, Ben?"

"I've got it under control, Peter. Glad you could make it."

"Wouldn't miss your annual bash."

Leah paused to kiss his cheek. "Hi, Uncle Peter."

"Hey, sweetie. I've missed seeing you around the office lately." He hugged Leah and leaned to kiss Marty's cheek. "Welcome home. I hear the trip was all you dreamed it would be."

Marty flashed him a happy smile. "And more. Thanks, Peter. You'll have to come over one night for dinner and look at the pictures. Ben took some interesting film footage as well."

"Interesting?"

"It's a bit choppy at the beginning but he got better toward the end of our trip."

"I'll do that."

Her father's partner glanced at the the Byrds, who were standing there. Leah introduced them. "Uncle Peter, this is Cecily Byrd and her son, Josiah."

He shook Josiah's hand and then held Cecily's hand for longer than expected. "Cecily. Pretty name for a pretty woman."

Leah saw Cecily color at his observation.

He lingered. "And how is it I've never met you at any of Ben and Marty's bashes in the past?"

"I only recently learned Leah was my old high school friend's daughter."

His brows lifted. "Let's get you a drink and you can tell me more."

Josiah watched helplessly as Peter ushered his mother away.

"Uncle Peter is okay," Leah said. "He's Daddy's partner at the clinic. Peter Leonard. He lost his wife to cancer about eighteen months ago. They were married longer than your parents."

Josiah's gaze followed the couple across the back yard. They stopped to pull sodas from a tub filled with ice, conversing as though they were lifelong friends. "I've never known Mom to act that way."

"Uncle Peter is good with people."

He looked at her. "Is he really your uncle?"

"No. We're not related. It's an honorary title. I've called him that since I was a little girl. He didn't like Dr. Leonard and Mom and Daddy wouldn't let me call him Peter so he came up with Uncle Peter. His wife was Aunt Molly."

Josiah rubbed his hands together. "Well, since my mother is in good hands why don't I offer my assistance in helping get these people fed?"

"That would be great, wouldn't it, Daddy?"

"I never refuse an extra pair of willing hands."

Marty picked up a tray. "Leah can help me bring the food out while you two finish up that batch. There's more in the fridge underneath the counter."

Inside, Marty looked at Leah. "Did you see the way she hugged your father? You'd think he was her best friend or something."

The burst of jealousy astonished Leah. Women often paid her father extra attention but her mother had never been bothered by the occurrences. "Cecily didn't mean anything, Mom. She's excited about seeing Dad. She even pulled out their old high school annual and showed me photos of Daddy with Joseph."

"I suppose she'll want to know why we didn't get in touch with them when we moved back to Wilmington."

"If she does, just tell her life got in the way. Uncle Peter sure took to her."

"Peter's lonely. He misses Molly and their kids rarely come to visit. I've been meaning to introduce him to the eligible women I know but apparently Cecily has caught his eye."

"You don't mind, do you?"

"It never hurts when two lonely souls find each other."

Leah wondered if her mother meant what she said. The partners and their families had always had a close relationship. What if Uncle Peter and Cecily became an item? Could her mother spend time with Cecily knowing she had been Joseph's wife? "So you're okay with Uncle Peter possibly dating Cecily Byrd?"

Marty crossed her arms over her chest and frowned. "I don't have a problem with Cecily Byrd or with any of the Byrd family for that matter."

Yeah, sure, Leah thought as she looked out the French doors to where Josiah and her father worked the grill. Their animated conversation was a good sign. "You think Josiah is okay with Uncle Peter? He's very protective of his mom."

Marty turned to look out the kitchen window. "Would you stop behaving like a mother hen? He's not chasing them around the lawn. No, wait. He glanced in their direction. He's going... Saved by your father. They're back to chatting."

Leah giggled at Marty's teasing play-by-play. "Leave it to you, Mom."

Marty cupped her daughter's cheeks in her hands and kissed her forehead. "Your friends will be just fine, Leah. Stop worrying and help me get this food out so the party can begin. We'd better hurry. Knowing your father, when it comes to interrogating your young men, Josiah needs rescuing by now."

They ate and mingled with the party guests. Leah was

happy to find Josiah knew some of their friends. She introduced him to her friends Susan and Carrie and their husbands. Carrie was interested in opening a retail storefront and Josiah gave her his card and told her to call him when she was ready.

The men went off for soda refills and both women turned to Leah.

"He's great."

"I like him," Susan said.

"Me, too." Leah admitted to her friends and herself. "I'm trying not to push the situation, though. We're taking our time getting to know each other."

"Is he the one?"

Susan's question forced Leah to consider the truth.

"He could be."

"Good. It's about time you found the man who deserves you."

"Let's hope he feels the same way."

Later, after their guests had gone, Leah and her parents settled in around the fire pit with Cecily and Josiah. Surprisingly Peter stuck around to listen while Cecily and Ben caught up on old times.

Leah felt sorry for her mom when Cecily's "remember when" stories, particularly those that had to do with her father's high school girlfriends, irritated her. Sensitive to his wife's feelings, Ben pulled her down next to him on the swing and placed an arm about her shoulders. She slumped against him, exhausted from the busy day.

Leah and Josiah sat in Adirondack chairs off to the side of the group. "You okay?" she asked softly when Cecily laughed at something Peter said.

He nodded. "Thanks for inviting us. Mom's having the time of her life."

"So you don't mind her and Uncle Peter? He is one of the good guys. When Aunt Molly got sick he stood by her through it all. He was at her bedside when she passed away."

Josiah's gaze rested on the couple. "Is he over her?"

Leah shrugged. "As much as one can get over losing someone they love. Those feelings never go away but others come into our lives and we move on."

"I like your dad."

"He's the best." Her fond gaze lingered on Ben Wright as he shared a story about a high school game he and Joseph played in. "You should listen to him. You might learn something you don't know about your dad."

His smile was forced. "It all comes back to the one I did know. No sense in hearing tales out of school and wishing that guy had stuck around to be a real dad."

Leah sighed. "Okay, have it your way." She pushed herself out of the chair. "Anyone want cake?"

Ben and Peter said yes. "Josiah?"

"I'll help."

She sliced cake, placed it on plates and added plastic forks. "Not birthday cake but Mom's icing is pretty good."

Josiah forked a bite in his mouth and nodded. "It bothers you when I put my father down. Why?"

Leah looked up at him. Had she been so obvious? "I hate to see you make yourself miserable."

She laid the knife back on the table and used a paper napkin to wipe away the excess frosting. Josiah sat his plate down and picked up a container of wet wipes. He pulled one out and handed it to her. "What do you mean?"

Leah wiped her hands and tossed it in the trash container. "He's gone, Josiah. He was your father and he was there for you. There are a lot of kids in this world who can't say the same. Kids who don't know who their father is. Kids who don't know where their next meal is coming from or where they're going to sleep tonight. Kids who would kill for a father, even a bad one."

"Easy for you to say. You scored father-of-the-year material."

Leah understood the hint of envy in Josiah's words. "I'm blessed. I know beyond a shadow of a doubt that my father would give his life for me. I'm not saying that to hurt you. It's just a fact I live with every day. And in some ways it's just as restrictive as the feelings you struggle with.

"It's like the love of Jesus. I can never totally deserve what He did for me. And nothing I do or achieve will ever put me in the paid column when it comes to all my parents have done."

"It's not an asset sheet, Leah. They love you. No matter what. You're their daughter, warts and all."

"Yes, but do you think that keeps me from wanting to make them proud, to give them something to brag about?"

"Your dad's plenty proud of his girl."

"And I'm sure your dad was proud of you. Maybe he didn't show it in the ways you expected but you can bet he bragged about you every time he got the chance. That's what parents do."

Josiah looked doubtful but Leah refused to relent.

"Hey, where's that cake?"

"Coming." She picked up two plates and indicated Josiah should take the remaining two.

Later, Josiah lay in bed considering what Leah had said that evening. Had his father bragged about his son? He thought about the things he'd done in his life to win his father's favor. The way he'd gone about it. As a kid, he'd idolized his dad. He'd trailed after him like a pup, tongue lolling and begging for a pat on the head. A good boy.

When that hadn't worked, he tried other ways. Rebellious acts that got him into more trouble than anything else. He'd finally seen the light when his mom sat him down for the talk. When she'd come to pick him up at the store, Mr. B. said he wouldn't file charges this time but if it happened again, Josiah would be arrested. She promised the store owner there would be no more trouble and yanked Josiah out of the store.

He hoped none of his friends had seen him that day as she grasped his hand in hers and pulled him along behind her all the way to her car. "Honestly, Josiah, if I could turn you over my knee and paddle you, I would. What were you thinking?"

He couldn't look her in the eye. Josiah had no idea why he'd let his friend prod him into taking the candy.

Cecily took him to the park and made him sit on a hard concrete bench while she paced and ranted. "You're making a major mistake and if you aren't careful you're going to do something that won't end with a stern talking-to."

He'd nearly cried like a baby when she told him she'd always been so proud of him and tears shone in her eyes when she added she'd never been as disappointed and angry as she was at this moment. "Do you think becoming a criminal will make your dad pay attention? It won't. He'll attempt to pay your way out and if he can't, he'll justify his actions by saying he's always worked hard to give you everything while *you* suffer the consequences of your actions."

Remorse filled him at her angry but sad words.

"Think about what you want from your future. Fortunately you won't have a criminal record because of this incident, but if you continue, your past will follow you wherever you go. It will tarnish every good thing you hope to accomplish and in the end you'll only be another spoiled brat who people will say doesn't deserve all you have. Is that what you want?"

That had been the breakthrough moment in his life.

His actions had hurt his mother and that was exactly what Josiah didn't want. She had loved him from the beginning. All his life, she'd been there for him and it was unfair to punish her and behave liked a spoiled child having a tantrum because he couldn't have a relationship with his father.

From that day forward, Josiah concentrated on making her proud. She'd cheered him on at team sports, been in the audience when he was recognized for his high school achievements and worked with him to complete his college applications.

He had his choice of colleges but instead of being pleased that he'd chosen UNC, his father took it as a personal affront. Each time he wrote a tuition check, Joseph made a big deal out of how hard he'd worked to get his scholarship and behaved as if paying Josiah's tuition was a major sacrifice.

Four years later when he received his degree, his parents had been there to see him graduate and his mother had been the one to make the event special by inviting his friends to join them for dinner.

Whatever the case, maybe Leah was right. His resentment of his father was a continuation of the resentment that fueled him to commit the rebellious acts of his childhood. Instead of showing the loving, lighthearted behavior his mom taught him, he became so bitter upon hearing his father's name that he couldn't say anything nice. He tried to cover his inability to forgive and forget by taking extra care with his mom and yet every time he flared up about his father, he hurt her with his behavior, just as he'd done as a youth.

Did his comments make him seem like an ungrateful brat? Probably. Leah made a good point. He'd never wanted for anything.

And every time he allowed those behaviors to surface he made his mother sad and upset just as he'd done that time all those years ago.

Josiah knelt and prayed for God's help with this burden

he carried. "Please, God, help me forgive my dad and please forgive me for being so resentful toward him. Make me a man deserving of the love You've shown me."

Chapter 11

The following Friday, Leah climbed behind the wheel of Josiah's truck. After adjusting the seat to her shorter legs, she reached for the rearview mirror. She hadn't particularly wanted to borrow the vehicle but Cecily insisted it would be easier to load the boxes. Leah knew that was true but she understood a man's feelings regarding his truck and feared she would be a nervous wreck until it was safely parked in the Byrds' driveway.

They were nearing the end of Cecily's project. She had decided to hold off on the attic, preferring to spend the time at the beach. She suggested she might want to resume working with Leah in the winter.

The reduced schedule and continued lack of new organization jobs prompted Leah to try other ways of earning money. She put together a leaflet of chores she would do, shared it with her fellow church members and posted it on the service board at the grocery store along with her cards.

Quite a few of the elderly members had benefited from

Leah's talents in the past when they did volunteer work at church. She'd worked in their homes, helping them sort and organize their things so they could find them and set up systems so they didn't miss their medications and appointments.

Those ladies called on her for help but she felt badly about taking their limited funds. Over the days she did grocery shopping, cleaned, walked dogs and even house-sat for dog owners. She accepted any errand that she considered an honest task and added to her bank account. The money wasn't as good as organizing but the extra funds in her bank balance made her feel more comfortable.

The dates with Josiah gave Leah hope for the future. She had fun whether it was working out at the gym or dining out. She'd noticed a difference in Josiah since the night of the party. He had stopped commenting on his father as much and Leah felt their bond strengthening.

She dreamed of a future with him. In her head, Leah could see them sharing a home, a life, and having a family together. She would even love her mother-in-law.

Josiah continued to surprise her on their dates. Some nights it was just dinner at one of the many restaurants in the city. One night they took a cruise along the Cape Fear River on the paddleboat called the Henrietta. They'd taken in more concerts. And some nights they'd walked along the beach or traveled to Topsail Beach to have dinner with his mom.

Cecily sipped from her coffee mug and set it in the cup holder to secure her seat belt.

"Whew. I haven't lifted boxes like that since I was a young woman."

Leah glanced at her. "I wish you hadn't lifted them today. You could have hurt yourself."

"Don't be silly. I nursed sick people most of my married life. They weren't exactly lightweights. A few boxes aren't going to be my downfall."

Cecily reached for her coffee and splashed it on the console and her pants leg. "Ugh. I knew I should have poured this into a travel mug."

She opened the glove compartment and rummaged for something to clean up the spill.

Leah's breath caught when she withdrew the flowered envelope that had become the subject of her nightmares.

"What is this?" Cecily read the return address aloud, a question in her voice as she turned the envelope over and noted the open flap. "Why did your mother write to Joseph?" She started to remove the letter.

"You don't want to read that." The words gushed from Leah.

Cecily's bemused expression contained much of the same concern Leah felt. What should she do? How could she handle this? She'd promised Josiah she wouldn't tell his mother about the letter but here it was with her demanding answers. Why hadn't he disposed of the letter as he'd said he would?

"I mailed it in error. I had no business messing with her things." The words ran together as Leah spoke fast in her effort to explain.

Cecily frowned. "You aren't making any sense."

Leah drew in a deep breath, fighting her desire to rip the envelope from Cecily's hands and shred it into a million tiny pieces. It was too late. The letter was in the exact place Josiah had never wanted it to be, right there in the hands of Joseph Byrd's wife.

"My mom wrote that letter before she started dating my dad. She kept it under her desk blotter. It's my fault." Her words came out sounding more like a sob.

"Leah, honey, don't cry. It's okay."

Cecily's reassurance made her want to cry harder. "No, it's not. When they were away, I planned to surprise Mom by doing a little organizing." Leah gulped back the dread that rose in her throat. "I was cleaning her desk. I thought she had forgotten to put it in the mail."

Cecily glanced down at the return label. "But she hadn't?"

Leah nodded, wishing they could backtrack to thirty minutes before when she'd stood in the kitchen telling Cecily to bring her coffee with her. She would have urged her to put it in a travel cup so there would have been no spill, no opening of the glove compartment, no finding that letter.

Total confusion showed in Cecily's expression and body language. "And you have no idea why she wrote Joseph?"

Leah shook her head. "I don't even know what it says. Josiah received it at the office. He was upset when he came to my parents' home to confront my mom."

"He did what?"

Leah grimaced, turning her head away as her eyes squeezed shut. What should she do? Cecily deserved better than lies and deception.

"He came to the house to confront Mom. To tell her his dad was dead. And how devastated you would have been if you'd received the letter.

"I knew Mom would never intentionally hurt anyone so I got her on the phone and she talked to Josiah. He calmed down after that. You know the rest of the story. While trying to explain what happened I gave him that business card you found and you called me."

Cecily fingered the envelope. "Why not destroy it?"

Again Leah shrugged. "I have no idea. That's why Josiah kept it. Said he planned to make sure no one ever saw it again."

Cecily's gaze fixed on her. "And you didn't read it?"

Leah looked directly into Cecily's cornflower-blue eyes, the same as her son's. "No. I told Josiah he shouldn't have, either. It's private."

Cecily held up the letter. "Between Marty and Joseph?"

"Yes, ma'am. Josiah says it's an angry letter."

"What's your mother's maiden name?"

"Washington. Her first name is Martha. She always got teased. That's why she calls herself Marty."

"Where did she attend college?"

Leah told her and Cecily said, "With Joseph and Ben."

"Surely Mom didn't know..."

"I doubt your mother knew I existed, just as I didn't know about her. Joseph made sure of that. In fact, I think he may have told me once that Ben had a girlfriend named Marty. You think she would talk to me?"

Leah shook her head. "She doesn't want to talk about the letter. I feel so bad. I never intended to cause this turmoil for her or for you and Josiah."

Cecily squeezed her shoulder. "Don't beat yourself up."

"Do you really want to know what it says?" Leah feared that whatever had happened between her mother and this woman's husband could cause Cecily anguish.

Cecily sat, lost in thought. For Leah, this was worse than her mother's anger.

"Leah, do you believe things happen for a reason?"

"Yes, ma'am."

"I do, too. I met Joseph when I was a sophomore in high school. He was a senior. I was wandering down the hall looking for my locker, not paying any attention to where I was going and ran into him. I fell down and he picked me up.

"From the first time I laid eyes on him I knew he'd be my husband one day. It broke my heart when he graduated and went off to college but I knew we'd be together. Just as soon as I graduated I'd join him at college and we'd be a couple again. Not two halves of a whole."

She laughed. "That's what I thought. We weren't whole without each other. He was my first love. My only love. My parents were very strict and I wasn't allowed to date for another year.

"Joseph and I saw each other at school every day and some of my girlfriends covered for us so we could go out. I'd never done anything like that. If you'd looked up good girl in the dictionary my picture would have been there, but this was different. I loved my parents but I loved Joseph more. I had to be with him.

"After he went off to college, I moped around home for months. They didn't know about Joseph but they agreed I needed to get out and socialize more. Said they were willing to let me start dating early. But I didn't want anyone else. I told Joseph I'd wait for him and that was exactly what I planned to do."

"Did you visit him at college?"

She shook her head. "I waited until he came home for the summer and brought him home to meet my parents. Mom and Dad had no idea. Joseph worked with his dad so except for a few days off when he arrived, he went to work every day and I waited for him to call. He grumbled all summer about having to work. He thought his dad should have let him hang out at the beach with his friends. I could tell things weren't the same but gradually we started hanging out again. Then summer was over. He left for college and I started my senior year.

"Joseph had pulled away even more when he came home for Christmas that year. He had so much in common with his college friends. A lowly high school senior didn't compare.

"But I hung on. I called and wrote and sent him care packages of his favorite cookies. I invited him to my senior prom and pleaded with him until he promised to escort me." Cecily sat, turning the letter over in her hands. "I never intended to trap him.

"We don't need to be Sherlock to deduce what happened. I think Joseph met your mother in college. I don't believe he cheated on me after we married but I do believe he took advantage of the opportunities to have other girlfriends when he was away at college.

"And if I'd been open to dating other guys, things would have been different for everyone. Just think, he might have married your mother and you would be his daughter."

Leah didn't think that sounded appealing at all. She made a mental note to give her father an extra hug next time she saw him. "You really believe Mom was his girlfriend?"

Cecily nodded. "Yes. I do. Seems my one-sided love affair with Joseph Byrd has hurt a lot of people." A tiny tear emerged and trickled along Cecily's high sculpted cheekbone. "Including my son."

Leah took Cecily's hand in hers. "Please don't cry. I do believe things happen for a reason. God didn't intend for him to be with anyone but you. You loved him and you were a good wife and mother. I know that. Not because Josiah tells me but because I can see the kind of person you are. Decisions were made by everyone involved and they were the right ones. You were married for over thirty years. A man doesn't spend that kind of time with a woman he doesn't love."

Cecily squeezed her hand. "Thanks, sweetie. College presented Joseph with a life he'd never experienced. Finally, he was free of his parents and free of me. He could do whatever he wanted." She lifted the letter again. "And if your mom wrote this letter in anger, he probably did things she never thought he'd do."

"You're not upset?"

She shrugged. "I suppose I could be but where do I direct that anger? Toward my dead husband? Your mother? Myself? His parents? What purpose would being upset serve? He's dead. I can't ask what he did and I don't think it serves any purpose to find out now. If I decide he did me wrong and spend the rest of my life as an angry, unforgiving widow, I'm the loser, not Joseph."

This response sparked hope in Leah. "That's what I want Josiah to understand. That anger hurts no one but him."

Cecily smiled broadly. "Just keep telling him that. And thanks for telling me the truth."

"Josiah has to grasp it for himself. I can't make him understand. As for the truth, he's going to be furious with me. He's been terrified the truth would come out. Terrified you would be hurt."

"We won't tell him I know."

That bothered Leah.

"I feel God brought you into our lives for a very specific purpose and if this letter guided you to us, thank God your mother wrote it. You're an answer to my prayers."

Not wanting Cecily to attach more to the situation, Leah said, "We're only dating."

"Are you attracted to Josiah?"

There were many things about him she liked. She had experienced something from the first time they laid eyes on each other. She hadn't wanted him to be angry with her or her mother. And she hadn't been able to forget him. She nodded.

"And he's attracted to you. One day my son is going to open his eyes and see what's standing right before him. He wants it all, the wife, the children and the home with the white picket fence."

"Isn't that a fantasy?"

"Not at all. When you really want something, you make it happen."

Leah wanted the same things. He'd once told her he didn't like her stirring up his world but he'd done some stirring of his own. And if Cecily was right and this was what God wanted for them, it could be for a lifetime.

"I hope your mom and I share more than Joseph."

Leah considered her own curiosity and wondered how Cecily could survive without knowing the truth. Particularly if that letter continued to surface at inconvenient times.

"Joseph was a good husband and provider. We were happy. He respected me as his wife and I respected him as my husband. We raised a fine son who I pray will one day give me grandchildren. That's what I look forward to now, Leah. The future."

"I'm sorry, Cecily."

Cecily eyed her crossly. "Do you have a Josiah complex? Are you trying to take the blame for something that happened before you were born?"

"If I'd left that letter alone no one would have known. Josiah would be moving on with his life just as you are."

"But you wouldn't be there. This is a good thing, Leah. And this letter is going to die with us." Cecily replaced the envelope in the glove box. "You should ask Josiah what he did with it and remind him to trash it before I change my mind."

"So you aren't going to read the letter?"

She shook her head. "As you said, it's private. I'd prefer to forget its existence."

"You think Josiah can?"

Cecily smiled slyly as she glanced sideways at Leah. "Maybe if someone gives him something more important to think about."

"Like what?"

Cecily laughed. "How much he loves you, of course. Now let's get rid of these boxes before I change my mind about them."

Leah managed a smile as she started the truck and drove away.

Chapter 12

As the days moved forward, Leah and Josiah managed to see each other a couple of times a week. One night, Susan and Eddie invited them over for a cookout. Afterward, they watched a movie and talked. Leah liked the way he fitted in with her friends.

Thanks to Cecily's referrals, Leah had picked up a few more jobs. No one wanted an extensive organization but she'd done a garage, a closet and a family room. One lady gave her sister a session with Clutterfree for her birthday. The sister took it well and they made great progress in her office.

Leah couldn't say for sure that she'd won the client over but she'd attacked the job with vigor and hadn't wanted to quit when their time was up. Leah suggested they continue but the woman couldn't pay her rate. Who knew? Maybe the sister would give her another day of organization for Christmas.

With the cutbacks at Cecily's, Leah worried but she had been able to pay this month's bills with a little money left over.

That afternoon Leah drove to her parents' house. They

were going to place Champ's ashes in the garden. She parked in the driveway and hit the trunk release. Cramming her keys in her pocket, she lifted her surprise. Holding the heavy package carefully, she closed the trunk and entered the backyard through the side gate.

Her parents were in the back corner under the shade trees, Champ's favorite place during the summer months. She placed the package on the ground and kissed their cheeks. Her father used the shovel to scrape back the mulch and dig a small hole.

"Are we sprinkling or burying?"

Ben shoveled the hole slightly deeper. "Burying. I loved Champ but I don't much care for the idea of him blowing in my face when I'm on the patio. What's in the package?"

Leah went down on her knees in the grass and turned it over so they could see. "I thought a stepping-stone would make the perfect marker for Champ."

Marty nodded. "That's lovely."

"I used the colorful stones to remind us of the joy he brought into our lives." She touched a ceramic butterfly she had included. "Remember how he loved to chase the butterflies?"

"And the birds," Marty reminisced. "I gave up hope of ever bird-watching again."

Ben nodded. "I spent many mornings drinking my coffee right here on this patio while Champ chased his nemeses. The squirrels loved to taunt him by running on the fence and up the trees. All he could do was bark and do that little jump of his. Kept thinking I'd film it sometime but never did."

Leah managed a teary smile as she traced her finger along his name.

Marty squeezed her daughter's shoulder. "It's perfect."

Each took turns sprinkling the ashes from the bag her mother had picked up from the vet's office.

"Does anyone want to say anything?"

Marty and Leah shook their heads, too choked up to speak. Ben took their hands and they all bowed their heads in silent prayer.

Afterward, he shoveled the dirt back in place and placed the stepping-stone over the spot. Then he arranged the mulch. "There. Rest in peace, old friend."

"Amen."

They walked back to the patio and Marty began deadheading some of the flowers they'd put out for the party. "These could do with water."

Ben pulled out the hose and showered the pots and beds. He playfully aimed the hose at Leah's bare feet. She'd shed her flip-flops in the lush grass.

"Daddy, stop. You'll get us wet."

He waggled the sprayer and grinned at her. Leah watched him as she stood and carried the handful of dead flowers over to the trash container and picked up the basket her mother used for the task. "Josiah said you two played a round of golf last week."

Ben nodded. "We did. He's good. He invited me the day of the party."

Her mother seemed to focus more on the work when she spoke. "Leah, your dad and I thought maybe you and Josiah would like to come for dinner Friday night. We could do something simple. Maybe steak, potato and salad."

Leah's heart gave a little leap of joy as she held the container so her mother could dispose of her debris. Marty moved to the next bed and began pulling weeds. "I'll ask. He likes steak. And I want you to get to know him better."

Marty looked up at her daughter. "So this relationship is serious?"

Leah shrugged, grinning happily as she threw her hands out, palms up. "I'm clueless. We enjoy spending time together.

Something I didn't think would happen after our first meeting. I'm so glad he's not holding a grudge."

"Not a trait you want in the man you love."

"Of course I don't know how he'll react to my most recent news."

Ben stopped weeding to look at her. "What have you done now?"

"I'm innocent this time." Leah shared the incident with Cecily and the letter. "She didn't read it. Cecily says not to tell him. I'm tempted. I know he's going to be furious when he finds out. He's been almost crazed with fear that it would happen."

"Maybe she has a point."

Leah eyed her dad. "You've always told me to tell the truth."

He nodded and rubbed his hand over his lower face. "And you should. I just hate that you'll be the one to suffer when it's not your fault."

Marty's gaze moved from her husband to Leah. "I agree. Josiah shouldn't blame you."

"His dad really did a number on him."

"I can't believe Joseph would treat his son like that. Doesn't sound at all like the young man we knew."

Leah stood and dusted her hands off. "Do you think maybe he changed after he came home? He and Cecily lived with the Byrds after they married."

Ben shook his head. "Poor Joseph. Jim Byrd had a one-track mind when it came to what he believed Joseph needed out of life. There was already a family business so in Jim's eyes he didn't need to waste his time with sports and college. Joe was pretty sure his parents wouldn't pay for him to go. He worked hard to get a scholarship."

Leah reached for one of the water bottles resting on the coffee table. She twisted off the cap and took a long drink.

"Cecily said her parents insisted that Joseph finish college so he could be a better provider for their daughter. They even paid for his education."

"I doubt that went over well with Jim," Ben said.

"And it was a waste since he went to work for his father anyway," Marty added.

Leah glanced at her mother. "I'm sure he learned enough business practices to make improvements in the business."

Ben grabbed a water bottle. After he downed half the bottle, he said, "If Jim let him. My impression was that he was one of those men who always believed his way was the only way."

"That must be where Joseph got it from," Marty said.

Leah glanced from her father to her mother. "Really? You saw that trait in him? I see it in Josiah at times. Particularly with this thing with the letter and his mom."

"Why is he so protective of her?"

Leah understood her mom's curiosity. "I really don't know. She's very self-sufficient. Cecily said Joseph's mom wasn't in the best of health and she cared for her and Josiah. I imagine they were all very close."

Ben nodded again. "Maxine had really bad asthma. Neither of his parents was overly friendly, but Maxine was the nicer of the two."

Marty dusted off her hands and picked up the third bottle. She dropped down into a chair. "That's a sad environment for a little boy."

"No way," Ben said with a hint of laughter in his voice. "Think one little boy with two doting women. You know they were intent on keeping Josiah happy."

"I think Cecily got more than she bargained for when she took Joseph on as a husband."

Marty looked surprised. "Did Cecily say that?"

Leah shook her head. "No. Never. Total assumption on my part. She loved him. Never dated anyone else."

"Joseph couldn't say that."

A definite chill crept into her mother's tone. Concern changed Ben's expression as he looked at his wife. Leah wondered how her dad felt regarding Joseph Byrd's ability to inspire anger in Marty after all these years. What was it about the man that stirred up the people she loved?

As she grew aware of their surreptitious looks, Marty spoke. "I'm sorry. I truly could care less about Joseph Byrd. It makes me furious that I allowed myself to be duped like that."

Confused, Leah asked, "Duped?"

Marty patted her daughter's hand. "It's not important, Leah. I thank God daily for my blessings." She glanced at Ben, love shining in her gaze. "And that He kept me from making a stupid decision all those years ago."

He winked at her and she winked back.

"Are you sure you want to invite Josiah to dinner?"

Marty's brown-eyed gaze fixed on her. "When you marry, your husband will become part of our family. Our son. And if God intends for Josiah to fill that role, we want to know and love him, too."

Leah wrapped her arms about Marty's neck. "I love you, Mom. I'll let you know what Josiah says."

As he drove over to pick Leah up for dinner with her parents, Josiah couldn't imagine what they had in store for him. Leah had said her mom asked about the seriousness of their relationship and that she had said they were enjoying getting to know each other. Josiah thought maybe Marty Wright might think he wasn't willing to commit.

Would it be the Wrights against the Byrd? The moment he let that thought into his head, Josiah struggled to squash it back. When had it become him and them? They had never been anything but hospitable. He couldn't judge them if he didn't want them to judge him in return.

He soon learned his fears had been in vain. Ben welcomed him and they talked golf over the grill as Marty and Leah prepared the sides. Over dinner, they laughed and talked like old friends. The conversation flowed from subject to subject with no uncomfortable pauses.

"You should have seen his face when they set his plate on the table," Marty said, struggling to hold back her laughter as she shared a story about her husband in a London restaurant.

Ben objected. "It's your fault. You were always telling me to be adventurous and try something different. I made a fool of myself."

She leaned over and kissed his cheek. "No, you didn't."

"We can't go back until they forget my face."

Marty hooted with laughter. "You'll never be forgotten."

Ben glared at his wife and she burst into laughter. "Honey, I'm sure you weren't the worst tourist they've ever had."

"Next to worst?"

Marty held back a guffaw. "I didn't say that."

Leah loved the way her parents teased each other. She stood. "I have a special treat for dessert. Daddy, will you help me?"

He laid his napkin on the table and stood. "Sure. I've taken all the abuse I can take from this woman."

When he stepped past her, Marty caught his arm and smiled up at him. "I love you, Ben."

He bent and kissed her. "I know."

"It's going to take a while," Leah warned.

After they went inside, Marty glanced at Josiah. "Think she planned this?"

He had zoned in on Marty Wright's discomfort almost from the moment they greeted each other. She treated him like a polite stranger, not exhibiting the same warmth he'd witnessed when she dealt with friends. Josiah understood. He felt similar stirrings. Doubts regarding her involvement with his dad. Her ability to ever accept him in her daughter's life. "Hard to say with Leah. You seem uncomfortable."

Marty paused briefly before she shrugged. "I suppose I am. Leah said you read the letter. I never planned on Joseph reading it, much less his son."

Josiah considered his reaction to the correspondence. "I was so shocked when it arrived on the anniversary of his death that I ripped it open and read without thinking. Then I raced over here to talk to you. I tried to get Leah to read it, too, but she refused. Said it's against the law to read other people's mail."

Marty smiled. "That's my Leah. I will admit that knowing you're privy to my deepest, darkest secret unnerves me. What did you take away from my letter?"

Josiah looked Marty in the eye. "That you were very angry and my father was a player. Given my existence, I think we can agree on obviously irresponsible."

"He married your mother."

"By choice?" The words came out sounding more like a challenge than a question.

Marty Wright shrugged. "Joe was always an enigma to me. When I tried to figure him out, he changed personalities."

They shared a common bond. Josiah had experienced his father's duplicity for himself. "He played games with people's lives."

Marty lifted her glass and took a long sip of the iced tea. "Maybe not. I think I assumed he committed when he really didn't. I realized that when he didn't return. Ben told me Joe had gotten married while they were home that summer. And that he and his wife were expecting. Once the news came out, I learned Joe had dated half the girls on campus.

"A number of young women believed they were his one

and only. He even dated one of my sorority sisters. She didn't know about me and I certainly didn't know about her. I couldn't believe I'd been so blind. Each time he said he needed to study was a date with another girl.

"But I was gullible. I can't tell you how many times I loaned him my notes when he missed an early class because of a late night. Or helped him research something when he was overwhelmed. I trusted him and for a few months after the truth surfaced, my biggest regret was not being able to confront him. Ben kept telling me I needed to forget and forgive. That's when I wrote the letter."

"You think it would have made a difference?"

When Marty tilted her head to one side and viewed him, Josiah wondered what she was thinking. "Not for him but it would have helped me. Joe never had regrets. No matter what happened, he put it behind him and moved on."

Josiah nodded agreement. "He just made everyone who knew him have them."

Marty nodded. "I poured out my heart in those pages, writing what I believed needed to be said to Joseph. Then I stuffed the letter in an envelope and decided to move on. Ben was a good friend and after a while we started dating. Turned out he'd wanted to ask me out but I chose Joseph."

"Rebound?"

She shook her head. "Never. I hate to think what I would have missed if I hadn't gone out with Ben. We've had our arguments but there's never been a moment I regretted marrying him. I kept that letter as a reminder not to hold grudges, to forgive and forget. Funny thing is I've pretty much forgotten what I wrote. My biggest regret is my own hypocrisy in not forgiving Joe."

That surprised Josiah. The vehemence in her writings struck him as the kind of thing a person would never forget. "He never mentioned my mom?"

Marty shook her head. "He never spoke of any other woman. When Joseph was with someone, she was his one and only. After the truth came out, I talked with some of the others and they all agreed. We could have started a recovery group on campus alone."

"And you didn't suspect?"

"No. That's what made it even more incomprehensible. I believed Joe to be an honest, upright young man who was going places. Then I found out he was a two-timing liar and cheat."

Josiah saw her struggle with the resurgence of anger the memories caused. Marty Wright regretted having known his father. "I'm sorry."

"You have nothing to be sorry for, Josiah. You're not your father and I can't blame you for his actions. I admit that what I knew about him makes me afraid for Leah."

Josiah felt as though the top of his head would blow off. "I have nothing but the greatest respect for your daughter. I wouldn't lead her on. And I'm not lying to her or cheating on her. We agreed that we want to get to know each other first."

Marty's gaze bored into him. "Respect?"

"I care for Leah."

"Like Joseph cared for me?"

Josiah ground his teeth. He wasn't Joseph Byrd. He was his own man and refused to allow this woman to compare him to his father's negative aspects. He knew what it was to love and be disrespected by the person he loved. To be dumped for someone they considered more to their liking. "As you've already pointed out, I am not my father."

"But you are his son. You've chosen the same college and operate the family business. Would you leave a young woman in pain because you decided you wanted someone else more?"

"You don't know me," Josiah growled the words. "I would never do anything like that to the woman I loved.

"I was invisible to my father. When he told me about the birds and bees, he said not to mess up like him and Mom. If I'd never been born, he'd have been happy. He provided financial support because my grandparents wouldn't let him do anything less. And if my mother hadn't loved him, I would have wished him out of my life forever."

Marty's sad expression spoke to him. "I'm sorry, Josiah. That's not what I'd want for any child. You deserve to be loved."

He corrected her misconception. "My mother loves me. She's loved me enough for both parents. I suppose she took the load on her shoulders for what happened but she believed dad loved her, too. That's why I have to protect her now."

"From what? Your father is dead. He can't hurt her."

"He can. The truth could devastate her. She loved him without fail. How will she deal with learning what he did after all these years?"

Marty leaned back in her chair and looked at him. "Your mom is stronger than you think. She had to be to survive her life. No mother can bear to see her child mistreated.

"As for Joseph, I think the freedom went to his head. I know it did for me. I wasn't wild with it but making your own decisions can be a heady experience. I had rules to live by but where I went and what I did was no one's business but mine."

"You think he tomcatted around because he was free to choose?"

Marty shifted uncomfortably. "I'm sure he cared for your mother, but absence doesn't always make the heart grow fonder. Suddenly he had dating options and no one to tell him no."

"He should have known better."

"What were you like when you went off to college?"

Josiah shrugged. "I went to college with my high school

sweetheart. Then she dumped me to run with the popular crowd."

Marty grimaced. "I'm sorry, Josiah."

He didn't want her feeling sorry for him. "Better before than after we were married."

Marty's brows lifted toward her hairline, her eyes growing larger. "You were that serious?"

"I probably would have married her eventually if she hadn't shown her true colors. She made me angry and, like you, I didn't wish her well. I started having so much fun that I nearly flunked out my first semester. Mom threatened not to pay my tuition if I didn't buckle down."

"Now that sounds like a normal college kid." She glanced toward the kitchen. "What do you think they're doing in there?"

He glanced over his shoulder. "Want me to go see?"

She shook her head. "Better not ruin Leah's surprise. So you're ready to settle down?"

"Yes. I'm thirty-two. Mom wants grandchildren."

"Did you choose Leah because you know she wants the same thing?"

She wouldn't give him a break. Nothing he'd said would convince her he had no intention of hurting her daughter. "I chose Leah because we have a number of things in common. I'm dating Leah because I like being with her. I wouldn't mind if it works out for us but we aren't rushing to the altar."

Marty looked suddenly apologetic. "Sorry if I came on too strong. Just promise me you'll be honest with her. Leah deserves that much."

He nodded. "I am honest with her. Our initial meeting resulted from an unintentional act on her part but I know she meant no harm. I truly like Leah. She's fun but we've shared some tough experiences with her helping Mom sort the house and your dog dying. I'm sorry about that."

Marty flashed him a sad smile. "Champ was an old dog. Still, it's like losing a family member. We buried his ashes over there under the trees." She indicated the area with a wave of her hand.

"Leah told me."

"Thanks for being there for her when she got the news. I wish we'd been home."

Those were the most sincere words she'd spoken to him. Josiah thought about what he was about to say. Marty should know her daughter had doubts. "She was very emotional. Took Champ's death personally. Said she'd let you down again."

Marty looked horrified. "We didn't blame her."

Josiah nodded. "I think she'd been feeling a load of guilt for mailing the letter, and losing Champ on her watch pushed her over the edge.

"There's something else going on with her. She's implied that she's not happy with the direction her life is taking. She hasn't said much. Just that the conversation was too heavy for a first date."

"Thanks for telling me. I'll talk to her."

Josiah leaned forward. "All I ask is that you give me a chance. Please don't think I'd ever do what my dad did to you."

"Can I make a suggestion?"

Josiah eyed her curiously. He shrugged. "Sure."

"I know you wish I'd never written my letter but it really did help me move on. As I wrote I understood things would never have worked out for us."

Where was she headed with this? She had been used by his father. Josiah doubted Joseph had any intention of marrying Marty or any of the others.

"You could write your own letter of closure to your dad. Tell him the things you've bottled up for years. Things you needed to tell him but didn't. It could help release the anger and free up this emotional logjam he caused in your life."

"I couldn't."

She reached over and gripped his hand, her voice strengthening with the encouragement. "You could. It's not that difficult. If it takes more than a letter, keep a journal. Or talk to someone. You're angry with him and it's eating at your happiness like water on stone. It will break you eventually if you don't let go. Believe me, I know."

Josiah frowned and she let go of her hold. "It's only a suggestion, but it does help."

"You said yourself he was an enigma. How would I ever share that?"

"You're not sharing. Just a private communication with your dad. It's not about what Joseph was. It's about how he affected you with his behavior. I know he didn't like opening up about his home experience. I got the impression his parents weren't easy people to live with."

"Grandma Maxine died when I was sixteen. I was twenty-four when Grandpa Jim died. Living with them helped acquaint me with their peculiarities.

"Grandma Maxine didn't spend a lot of time with Dad. She spent most days in her bedroom. When Grandpa couldn't work anymore, he told Dad what to do in the business and when I went to work there Dad tried to order me around. But he had nothing to hold over my head. He couldn't fire me. Grandpa wouldn't have let him. And I had my own condo. I moved out of their house as soon as I possibly could.

"I have Grandma Maxine to thank for that. When I was little, she'd have Grandpa leave all his pocket change every day. We spent hours feeding her old tin collector's banks. They fascinated me as a kid. I still have them.

"Instead of putting the money in over and over, she added more every day. When the banks were full, the money came out and went into an account that had been set up for me. Then when she died, she set aside another amount for me to use as a down payment on my first place."

"Why did you go into business with your dad?"

That was a question Josiah had never been able to answer. With a business degree he could have done anything, but his grandfather was showing his years. When Grandpa Jim asked him to carry on his legacy, Josiah had done the course work, passed the exam and become a licensed real estate broker.

"Because Grandpa asked me to. Turned out I was pretty good at sales."

"Better than your dad?"

It shamed Josiah somewhat to admit that at times he had turned the company into an in-your-face experience for his dad. He loved to rub it in when he made deal after deal, particularly when clients preferred dealing with him over the senior Byrd.

"Yeah. I have my mom's personality. She can talk to anyone about anything. She took me places and introduced me to people. I'm good with names and faces, and clients loved it when this kid they'd known all his life came on the business scene. They remembered me. Still do. Anyway, when they were looking to buy real estate, they called me."

Marty smiled at him. "Your mom did a great job raising you, Josiah. I look forward to knowing you better."

"So have I alleviated your concerns about me and Leah?"

"Let's say I see you in an entirely different light and I'm beginning to like what I see."

"Works for me."

As if they'd timed their exit Leah came out, holding the door for her dad who carried a tray of ice cream sundae ingredients. She placed the ice cream churn cylinder on the table. "Oooh, cold." Leah blew on her hands and did a little dance. "You're about to taste the best peach ice cream you've ever had." She took the scoop from the tray.

Marty smiled at Leah. "We wondered what you two were doing. It's been forever."

"We haven't made ice cream all summer."

Josiah thought she sounded like a disappointed little girl. She held the scoop over the container. "Josiah?"

He nodded and she placed two large scoops in his bowl. She indicated the sundae items. "Help yourself."

"You know I prefer my ice cream plain."

"Coward."

Leah liked extras on her ice cream. She had taunted him about adding this or that on the numerous times they'd gone out for ice cream but he'd stuck with plain ice cream.

"Mom?"

"Just one scoop for me. I've indulged far too much lately. My clothes are getting tight."

Leah filled her father's and then her own bowl and they dithered over the items before settling on their preferences.

"Mmmm. Scrumptious," she declared after swallowing the first bite.

"Best ice cream I've had all summer." Ben spooned another bite into his mouth.

Leah waved her spoon at her mother and Josiah. "So did you two get a chance to talk?"

Josiah glanced at Marty Wright. "We did."

Leah smiled. "Good. I want my favorite people to like each other."

Later, after they said their good-nights and walked out to his truck, Leah was fastening her seat belt when Josiah reached to open the glove compartment. He pulled out the letter. "I'll be right back." He jogged to the front door and rang the bell. Ben answered and they disappeared back inside.

Minutes later, when Josiah climbed back into the truck, Leah asked, "What was that about?"

He started the truck. "Just returning something to its rightful owner. I'm glad to have it out of my possession. Maybe now I can stop worrying."

"So you gave the letter back to Mom? I hope she locks it up or runs it through the shredder."

"It's her property, whatever she decides to do with it, though I do suspect she'll put it out of the way of prying hands and eyes."

"I wasn't prying."

"Okay, your helping hands and my prying eyes."

As they drove toward her condo, Leah's heart grew heavy. Cecily had said they weren't going to mention what happened but how could she not? She couldn't keep secrets and expect him to trust her. "Josiah?"

"Hmm?"

"I have to tell you something."

He turned the radio down. "What's that?"

Leah swallowed hard and started talking before she lost her nerve. "Cecily knows about the letter. She found it when we used your truck the other day. She had questions and I answered them."

Josiah stomped on the brakes and wheeled into a parking lot. He reached up and turned on the interior light. "You did what? Why didn't you tell me before? What do you mean you answered her questions? You don't even know what it says." He saw the way she backed away from him.

"She didn't read the letter."

"How did she find it?"

"She spilled her coffee and was looking for a napkin. I almost died when I saw what she had in her hand."

He slammed his palms against the steering wheel, feeling

the sting as they hit the hard rubber. "I knew I should have thrown that thing away."

"She didn't read it."

Why did she keep repeating that? Did Leah think it mattered? "I don't care. She'll fret over the contents and make herself miserable. I knew this would happen. Mom's the only person in the world I need to protect and I can't even do that."

"Cecily doesn't need protection. She's stronger than you think."

"What is it with you Wright women? You and Marty don't know anything about my mom. Or me, for that matter. I trusted you, Leah. You promised not to tell her."

"What was I supposed to do? Smack her hand and tell her to put it back?"

"Don't be facetious. It doesn't become you."

"Well, you're being ridiculous and it doesn't become you, either. Ask your mom what happened. She'll tell you."

"Just forget it. This is exactly what I knew would happen."

He pulled out into the street and drove directly to her condo and left the engine running.

"Aren't you coming in to discuss this?"

He wouldn't look at her. "No. I'm going home. I need to think about how I can fix this."

"There's nothing to fix. Cecily isn't as heartbroken as you seem to think."

"You can't understand."

"I guess I can't. Good night, Josiah."

She got out and he drove away without a word.

Chapter 13

Leah accepted the check her father handed her. She'd worked in the office a couple of days and the money would get her through another month.

It was late and they were in Ben's office. Leah propped against the large executive desk as he worked at his computer. Everyone else had gone for the day. "What happened between you and Josiah?"

It had been a week since the dinner and he had not called in that time. Leah had considered contacting him, trying to explain again that nothing happened, but she found herself resenting Josiah's behavior. And that comment that his mom was the only person in the world he needed to protect. If he cared, he would feel the same about her.

She shrugged. "I haven't heard from him. I guess he's still thinking about how he can fix things."

Ben leaned back in his chair and frowned up at her. "Fix what?"

"This thing with Cecily finding the letter."

Concern flashed onto Ben's face. "You told him?"

Leah nodded. "He was totally unrealistic. It was his glove compartment. What was I supposed to do? Here's this letter to her husband with my mom's name on the return label. Surely Josiah didn't think I could blink my eyes and, poof, it's gone." She shoved her hair over her shoulder. "I told her Josiah would be upset. Now he doesn't trust me."

"Seems he must be pretty angry if he's not seeing you."

Leah had spent hours trying to understand Josiah's concern. Did he really think Cecily had no idea of the kind of man her husband had been? Could a woman spend more than thirty years with someone she loved and not know everything about him?

"What are you going to do?"

She shrugged. "Not much I can do. He says I don't understand and I really don't. He's obsessed with this situation. He called the letter our secret. I told him from the beginning that I would not lie. He's the one who stuck it in the glove compartment."

"But you were the one who mailed it." Her father reminded Leah of her role. "Are you still working with Cecily?"

"We're finished. I don't think she knows Josiah and I aren't dating each other."

"She and Peter are seeing each other pretty often."

A jolt of happiness for Cecily shot through Leah.

"He's driven over to Topsail Beach to take her out to dinner a few times. And he's met her new friends and really likes them."

"At least one Byrd is moving on with life. I hope they make each other happy. Cecily is a sweet lady."

"They clicked right away."

Leah nodded agreement. "I saw Uncle Peter's reaction."

Her dad dug through the stack of folders. "It's good to see him happy again. Any movement on the job front?"

She shook her head. "Not lately. I guess Cecily ran out of friends or else the others aren't interested in organization."

"What will you do?"

Leah considered the thoughts that had filled her head. Maybe it was time to share them with her father and see what he recommended. "I think it's time I found a real job."

Ben looked concerned. "Are you in trouble financially?"

She waved the check. "The bills are paid this month but I'm tired of living this hand-to-mouth existence. I need to find something with benefits and get myself a retirement plan going. I'm not getting any younger."

"Do you have any savings?"

"Not really."

Her dad looked thoughtful. "I've been meaning to talk to you. Josiah told your mom you got very emotional when Champ died and said you felt you'd let us down. You didn't blame yourself for that, did you?"

Leah felt her skin color. "I suppose I did. You planned the trip of a lifetime and here I am at home sabotaging everything."

"Champ was old, Leah. What's really going on?"

"I've been praying and reading my Bible and trying to understand why I don't feel I've accomplished anything worthwhile with my life."

Her words put him up in arms. "How can you say that? You're a wonderful person. A wonderful daughter."

"And you're my father. You're expected to say things like that, but what have I ever done to really make you and Mom proud?"

"We love you, Leah."

"I'm twenty-eight years old. I should at least have a good-paying job and a significant other in my life. I felt such hope when Josiah and I were together. For a while, I thought that just maybe God had sent the man He intended for me. But he wasn't. That man wouldn't turn his back on me for such a stupid reason."

"Perhaps it's not stupid to him."

His comment hit Leah hard and she nearly cried as she considered her unworthiness. "I know. I've downplayed this to keep myself from feeling so bad about what I did."

"Everyone makes mistakes, honey. That's part of life."

"It's just another excuse, Dad. It frustrates me that I live in a one-bedroom condo, drive a leased car and I'm holding on by the skin of my teeth in hopes that I won't be one of those adult kids forced to move back home."

"You're always welcome."

"I know. But I need to do something meaningful with my life. Something that will make you and Mom beam and say that's my girl."

"We do that all the time. You're well-loved by the people who count you among their friends. Not to mention the adults who watched you grow up."

She flashed him a self-deprecating smile. "Please, Daddy. When you were my age, you were a dentist, husband and father. Mom was a loan officer, wife and mother. She worked to support the family while you got your degree. Neither of you opted to live from paycheck to paycheck like I do."

He snorted. "We haven't always had money in the bank. There were lean times when I was in school. Your mother worked hard and dealt with her guilt over putting you in day care and I dealt with mine over her having to work. It wasn't easy but we survived. And since we never had another child it benefited you to socialize with children your age."

"You've been wonderful parents. I'm blessed to have you in my life. I just want to be a better daughter."

She had never seen him look so nonplussed.

"What do you want me to do, Leah? Push you out of the

nest? Shove you out of your comfort zone and shout 'Go forth and spread your wings'?"

Leah smiled at his dramatic waving of his arms. "I don't think we need to be quite that symbolic but the time has come for me to take a big step forward in life."

Determination set his strong masculine face. "Then do it. There's nothing you've ever set your mind to that you didn't accomplish."

Love for him filled Leah. Her parents were so wonderful. She wished Josiah could have had a dad like hers. He would have been a different man.

"Did you read Mom's letter?"

He shook his head. "It was personal. After Josiah gave it back to her, Marty reread the letter for the first time since she sealed that envelope over thirty years ago. She shared some of what she said but deemed it stupid and petty on her part. Said she sinned by not forgiving Joe. Her inability to forgive him has worried her for years."

Leah nodded. "Mom always stressed forgive and forget."

"Probably because she saw it as a weakness in herself. Joe Byrd embarrassed Marty. Her first college boyfriend made a fool out of her.

"When I told her why Joe wasn't coming back, she poured out her frustrations. She needed to talk and I was willing to listen."

"She should have confronted him."

"Marty knew it would serve no purpose. Joe wasn't the type to say he was sorry. And she didn't feel it would be fair to his wife. I told her she needed to let go of the anger. But she was humiliated. Marty spent that entire semester fuming over Joseph Byrd."

"And that didn't bother you?"

"I felt her pain. I was angry with Joe for making her sad.

I stood by for more than two years while she treated me like a brother."

Leah's eyes widened. "A brother? Really?"

He chuckled. "Well, we did flirt a lot. She introduced me to her friends and they told me Marty said I was handsome and smart."

"So she compared you to Joseph Byrd and you scored top of the list."

He shook his head. "I don't think she did. When I kissed her that first time, she said she was so glad none of her friends had snapped me up. I like to believe she came to love me for who I am. Not for who I wasn't."

Leah sighed heavily. "I caused so many problems."

"It wasn't intentional. This has never been an issue in our marriage, Leah. I love your mom and we're very happily married. Joe Byrd has been nonexistent to us, but now that there seems to be a Byrd around every corner, we have to deal with the situation."

"And you weren't troubled that Mom didn't choose you first?"

Ben grinned, shaking his head at her persistence. "Girl, you're like a dog worrying a bone with that question. I got the girl I loved and that's all that matters. I was her friend and then our love grew. We've been very happy and that love will continue until death do us part.

"God sometimes has a way of forcing the issue. Joseph Byrd's name has been mentioned in my house more in the past couple of months than in all the years we've been married. Marty's not wearing her heart on her sleeve for him. He hurt her pride. No one likes being deceived by a friend."

"What kind of man was he?"

"We were kids, Leah. Self-centered jocks who were more interested in playing football and chasing girls than exploring the depths of our souls.

"Joe's parents weren't very supportive. He always said he was going to be the best and make them see what they had missed. When Joe got the scholarship, Jim made it clear that he thought it was a waste of time. Joe saw the scholarship as an out. It got him away from his parents but deep down inside he knew what he would do. Then he dug himself into another hole. Some would say he was a no-luck-at-all kind of person, but he was more of the leap-before-he-looked type.

"Cecily was young when they met and she was his biggest, most devoted fan. For her, the sun rose and set in Joe. But she was a good girl and he was a frustrated boy."

"He wasn't a believer?"

"No. My parents warned me about him all the time. Everyone considered Joseph a wild child and they thought he would get me into trouble. I kept my head screwed on right and didn't let him lead me down the wrong path. I defended him when they said those things because he was my friend."

"Why wouldn't he love his son?"

"I suspect Joe loved him in the only way he knew how. He provided well for his family."

"I hate it for Josiah. I wish him nothing but happiness."

She'd struggled with her feelings. Cried her tears in private and decided there was no way she could change the situation.

"That's my girl. And that's the sort of thing that makes me beam. Your mother and I are proud of the person you've become."

"Thanks, Daddy." Leah picked up a framed photo of her parents in front of the Eiffel Tower. "This is new."

"Your mom gave it to me. It's her favorite photo from our trip."

She glanced around at the other photos in the room. Her mom, Leah with her mom, family shots of the three of them and her dad beaming as he held his infant daughter.

Leah longed for photos like these.

"So what are you going to do about these doubts of yours?"

She turned back to her dad. "Set some goals and write them down. Susan said she read that people who did were usually successful. Then I'll get my résumé together and hopefully find a job that fulfills me as much as organization does."

Ben stood and hugged his daughter. "I pray for you always, honey. That God will give you to the happiness you deserve. Your mother and I are willing to help if you decide you want to return to school."

She hugged him back. "Thanks, but it's past time I utilize the education you've already paid for and find myself a job." The large pendulum clock on his wall chimed the hour. "You'd better head for home. Mom's going to be wondering where you are."

Ben hugged her one last time. "Let me know if I can help."

On the way to her condo, Leah picked up a sub sandwich and a newspaper. She let herself in and grabbed a bottle of green tea from the fridge. While she ate, Leah glanced through the classified ads, not surprised when nothing appealed to her.

She went to her desk and pulled out her ideas for her thesis. It had been a while since she last looked at them. All she lacked in obtaining her master's was the thesis. She couldn't believe she'd allowed herself to get sidetracked that year. She'd gotten pneumonia and it lingered on. The doctor had suggested she take a break and that break had extended for years instead of months.

After a few pages, the feeling it was trash overcame Leah and she pushed it aside in favor of perusing employment sites on the computer. She read ad after ad, none of which would have appealed to her even if she were qualified.

Maybe now wasn't the time to do this, Leah thought. But

then there had never been a good time to pursue her future and what she hoped to accomplish with her life.

Her thoughts drifted in a natural progression from the conversation with her father to Josiah and what he was doing. In a short time, she'd come to hope he might be part of her future. It hurt that he hadn't trusted her when it came to protecting Cecily. She would never intentionally hurt anyone and especially not someone she liked as much as Cecily.

He'd been so unrealistic. Once his mother knew the letter existed, it couldn't be ignored. The truth had kept Cecily from reading the letter. Leah didn't regret what she'd done nor would she be made to feel guilty by Josiah.

His father may have spent his life trying to escape. Maybe he was unhappy because of what happened. Whatever the case, he had accepted his responsibility and provided well for his family. That had to mean something.

Chapter 14

Josiah tossed down his pen in disgust. Ever since Marty Wright suggested he write down his feelings, he'd toyed with the idea, scribbling a thought and then running it through the shredder behind his desk.

He stood and walked to the window, staring blindly at the wooded area behind the building. His dad had made an effort to improve the view by making the small area for the employees. The smokers used it more than anyone else.

This was his father's world. Josiah still wondered why he'd made the move. No reason except his staff had said he should relocate into the big office. The furniture was the best money could buy, the carpet a plush pile that cushioned his footsteps. The walls and the hutch had been filled with tributes to his dad before he'd had them packed away. The only photo in the room was of his mother. The one his father kept there. No photos of father and son in this room.

Would writing down his angry thoughts help him? Would

the angry commentary to his dead father serve any purpose? Could he write the things he'd never shared in real life? Things his dad wouldn't have heard even if he had said them?

The office door swung open and Cecily Byrd marched into the room. "What's going on, Josiah?"

His assistant trailed after her. Josiah waved her off. He ripped the page off the legal pad and balled it up, tossing it into the trash can.

Cecily rarely came to the office but evidently had something on her mind today. He stood and stepped around the desk to kiss her cheek. Josiah lifted one dark brow and looked at her. "You want to give me a clue as to what you're talking about?"

She kissed him back. "Peter said you and Leah aren't dating any longer. Why didn't you tell me?"

He towered over his petite mother. "I haven't seen you. And since when have you kept track of my relationships?"

Offended, she said, "I am not keeping track. I consider Leah to be my friend."

He shrugged. "We had a difference of opinion."

"Trust issues?"

Leah must have told her parents the whole story. "Yeah. Something like that."

Cecily went on a rant. "Does it have anything to do with that stupid letter? I should have known she'd tell you. Leah isn't capable of deception, Josiah."

His mother's rambling made him feel even worse about the way he'd treated Leah. "This is not your concern, Mom."

"It is if you're trying to protect my feelings. Leah didn't know what was in the letter, but you do. Tell me what has you so upset."

He had to get her off the subject. "It's nothing, Mom. Tell me about you and Peter."

"Other than the fact that I haven't dated since high school

and it's really strange to be seeing someone at my age, I like Peter. He's a great guy. He lost a loved one to cancer so we share that."

"And you really like him?"

She nodded. "He called the day after the party and asked me out. We've seen each other often. My friends at the beach love him."

"You're a beautiful woman. I'm sure he's proud to have you on his arm. But how do you feel?"

"Both flattered and unsure. I loved Joseph but I didn't die with him. I was lonely but Peter and my new friends make me feel more alive than I've felt in a long time."

"So your changes have been good ones?"

"I believe they have. I know I owed it to Joseph not to rush out and get involved with another man but I feel I waited a suitable time."

"Definitely. No one's going to criticize you for your decisions and if they do it's not their concern. You're entitled to your happiness. I'm behind you all the way."

"Thanks, sweetie. I feel better knowing you're okay with my choices."

"You don't need my permission to live your life, Mom."

"I care what you think and feel, Josiah. Now tell me why."

He knew he couldn't waylay her for very long. She had come to Wilmington with a mission in mind and wouldn't leave until she understood what was going on with him.

Josiah sighed heavily. What was it with these women? Marty Wright had questioned his intentions and now his mother was doing the same thing? Didn't they understand men didn't wear their hearts on their sleeves? "It wouldn't work."

"What do you mean?"

"It just wouldn't, Mom. I'm not about to saddle Leah with a jerk like me. Now let it go."

She clutched his lower arms and stared up at him. "You aren't a jerk. You were a sensitive little boy who has turned into a sensitive man. Your father and I were kids. Too immature to be parents."

Josiah couldn't make her feel bad. She'd been an excellent mother. "You did a good job."

She flashed him a loving smile. "Thank you. I need to know what the letter said. I have to understand why you felt the contents would devastate me."

"I can't." Silently, he begged her to understand.

Cecily sat down on the sofa in the office and dropped her large purse onto the floor next to her. "You have to. It's eating you alive and I'm not leaving until you tell me. Either that or I'll ask Marty Wright to share the letter with me."

And she would, Josiah thought. Out of love for him she'd march over to the Wright home and speak to Marty mother-to-mother. "It was an angry missive. After he didn't return to college, Marty learned Dad had dated other women. She thought he loved her."

"I see."

"You see that good old Dad was a player?"

She shook her head. "He was a free agent, Josiah. There was no engagement, no promises for the future. My only hope was that we would rekindle our high school relationship when we met up again in college."

The next question was so hard to ask. "Did you get pregnant to hold on to him?"

"I understand why you might feel that way, but no. You were created out of a young girl's love for her boyfriend and her hope for a future with him. He didn't take anything I didn't give out of that same love."

He nodded. He'd never understand his mother's feelings for his father, the reason she'd given so much of her life for him. But he couldn't keep rehashing this. He had to let it go.

Josiah knew one thing in that moment. He would not be like Joseph Byrd. He would not allow the man who had controlled people like puppets to have the upper hand.

"You owe Leah an apology. She was devastated when she saw what I held. I thought she would cry. When I started to pull it from the envelope, she almost jumped me right there. She told me I didn't want to read the letter. She didn't worry that I might be upset with her mom. She worried about you. I encouraged her to let this be our secret. But she couldn't. She knew she'd lose your trust if you found out."

"And she did. All I could think about was what you would do when you learned your husband had played the field in college. You gave so much and I wanted you to be happy."

"Sweetie, your father made me happy. You made me happy. I got exactly what I wanted out of life. He once told me both of you benefited from my abundance of love. I think that's the nicest thing he ever said to me."

He knew he'd treated Leah badly. She'd repeatedly told him Cecily hadn't read the letter but the red haze in his mind couldn't take in anything except the fact that his mother knew.

"Josiah, how do you really feel about Leah? If you put the letter and all that confusion about your dad behind you, what do you feel?"

He sat down on the sofa next to her. "She's one of the most standout women I've ever known. Leah inspires and challenges me at the same time. When I'm mired down in my self-pity she tells me to get over it. She says I'm blessed just to have parents and grandparents who took care of me.

"She's not into possessions, and money seems to be important for survival only. Our dates were always simple and fun. Whenever I did something special to impress her, she took it in stride. Never insisted I spend more and more."

Cecily nodded agreement. "Leah showed a lot of heart

when helping me. Some organizers would have demanded I throw everything away, but not Leah. She's good at that job."

He smiled slightly. "I think Leah changed because of you. She said we threw our memories away with both hands while you treasured them. Thought you probably had the right idea.

"Marty Wright suggested that I write a letter to Dad. Express my thoughts and emotions and seal them away like she did."

His mother's gaze didn't leave his face. "I'd rather you forgive your dad. It's time to stop dwelling on what could have been. Accept it for what it was and make your future what you want it to be. You spent so much time with women. There wasn't a male around to teach you to be a man."

"Well, Mr. B. certainly gave me what for when I tried to shoplift from his store. I thought he was going to have me arrested but he took me into his office and said you would be sad that I had done that. He didn't say anything about Dad or Grandpa, just you.

"That was when I accepted how good my life had been because you had been there for me. You made my life better."

She wrapped her arm about his and hugged it to her. "There's so much I wanted, still want, for you. And you can have it all."

"I know, Mom."

They hugged and Cecily leaned back, using her fingers to wipe away her tears. "The only advice I have for you is to do what you need to do. The decisions are yours to make. The future is yours to take. Now I'm going to the house to change. Peter is picking me up later and we're going to see a play at Thalian Hall."

The beautiful old theater downtown was one of the best things in Wilmington.

"Enjoy yourselves. Tell Peter hello for me."

She chuckled. "I think he was sorry he said anything about

you and Leah. He didn't think this was a good idea. Maybe he was right and I shouldn't have come."

"I'm always happy to see you, Mom. I love you."

She caressed his cheek. "I love you, too, my sweet boy."

Cecily's words lingered long after she left. Josiah knew there was no need to write a letter to his father. He wouldn't spend the rest of his life trying to understand his father or wishing for something he would never have. As Leah had once said, there are no do-overs in life.

He could change his life. Become a man his mother would be proud to have as a son. And become a loving husband to a wife and a great father to the grandchildren she insisted on.

With God's help, he could do all those things. He only had to ask to receive.

Chapter 15

Leah stuffed the final pieces of clothing in the suitcase and pressed down in an effort to close the zipper. When it didn't work, she pulled the bag onto the floor and sat on it, smiling victoriously when the zipper slid closed.

She stood the case up and pulled other items from about the room. She even took the little Eiffel Tower her mom had given her. For some reason she'd begun to see the souvenir as a goal for her future. One day she would see it for herself. Leah bubble-wrapped and packed her treasures in the boxes she used for organizing the homes of others. These were the things she planned to take with her.

When Leah thought about finding a job, she'd never imagined she would be successful so soon. Actually, she hadn't done anything but visit Susan. Her friend had missed church for the past week and she stopped by to see what was going on.

"Come on in. I'm fine." Susan grinned and said, "It's morning sickness. But it's lasting all day."

Puzzled, Leah repeated, "Morn… You're pregnant?"

Her friends had wanted a child for years. Susan nodded, a big smile on her face. "We couldn't believe it. I thought I had a stomach bug."

Leah hugged her. "I'm so happy for you both."

Susan settled on the sofa, propping up her swollen feet. Leah sat in the armchair.

"And you're really okay?"

"I saw the doctor today and he's warned me to take things slow and easy. Have you heard from Josiah?"

Leah shook her head. "Not one word."

"I can't believe he'd act like this. He seemed like a really decent guy."

She couldn't help herself. Leah had to defend Josiah. "I couldn't believe he'd act that way either until Daddy pointed out that this is significant to Josiah. He's right. I can't discount the importance of the situation. If I hadn't mailed that stupid letter, none of this would have happened."

Susan eyed her. "What will you do?"

"I enjoyed my time with Josiah. He holds a special place in my heart and I wish things could be different but it's doubtful things will change for us. Meanwhile, I have to find work."

"Organizational?"

Leah shrugged. "I'd love nothing more but the jobs aren't there. I've been reading the classifieds and looking online but there's not much out there. I'm trying to formulate a plan but it's slow going. I need a full-time job."

The phone rang and Susan gestured for her to hang on.

"Kimmie. I'm so glad you called. I know. Can you believe it?"

Kim was Susan's older sister who lived in Atlanta. Leah knew her on that level but they had also shared a few college classes and connected. Kim had gotten her master's and now worked in the human resources office of a large business.

"Leah's here. I just told her our news. She's fine. Looking for work."

Susan listened to her sister. "No. She says she can't find anything. Hang on. I'll tell her."

"Kim says there's a job posted on their website that would be perfect for you. Take a look and give her a call."

"Tell her I will. Thanks."

She had returned home, checked the website and called Kim early the following morning.

"It's time management training with an emphasis on organization. You can use your expertise and experience to do what they need. I had told my boss about you and he said it was a shame that you didn't live in Atlanta. I didn't call because I figured you and Susan were permanent fixtures there in Wilmington."

Leah's preference would be to remain in Wilmington. "You really think I could do what they want? I've worked mainly in clients' homes. Not businesses."

"I know you can. It's a temporary position. Only two months, but it would look good on your résumé. You can stay in my spare room as long as you want. You'll have time to sort things out and decide if this is something you want to pursue."

Leah couldn't believe this had happened. She knew God had answered her many prayers. "Oh, thank you, Kim. I knew I would probably have to leave the area but being there with you will make it easier."

"It's hard stepping out on your own. I felt the same way when I first came to Atlanta. But I've never regretted my decision."

Leah prayed she wouldn't regret hers. "I really need to do this. I've been playing at supporting myself when in reality my parents have been helping me all along. I doubt Daddy needed help at the office as often as he called me. So where do I send my résumé?"

"Hold on a sec."

She listened to the jazzy tune that played as she waited for Kim to return.

"Sorry. I wanted to check with my boss. He said if you fly in on Thursday afternoon, he can meet with you on Friday morning? You can bring your résumé and learn what they expect. Then you can make the decision."

"Kim, you are a lifesaver."

"So you'll come?"

"Yes. Definitely."

"Great. Can you stay over the weekend? I'd love to show you around."

Leah had barely arrived home on Monday when they called and offered her the job. They wanted her to start work the Tuesday after Labor Day. She'd begun making arrangements almost immediately after telling her parents. She was scared. Leah couldn't lie about that. Leaving them behind would be the worst part but they agreed she was doing the right thing.

Her heart hurt at the thought of never seeing Josiah again but Leah accepted that things weren't going to change. She couldn't be what he needed her to be.

Tomorrow morning she would leave for Atlanta. Leah would settle in at Kim's and prepare to start work on Tuesday. The prospect of her new life alternately thrilled and frightened her.

Because the position was temporary, Leah would hold on to her condo until she had a permanent position.

She glanced at her watch. Time to get a move on. She'd told her mom she'd be at their house by five and she still had to pack her car and do a few more things. She'd have dinner with them, spend the night and say her goodbyes early the next morning.

But there was one last thing she had to do.

Leah sat down at her desk and pulled a sheet of stationery from the drawer. She picked up her pen and wrote, the words pouring from her almost faster than she could write them down.

After she finished, she reread the last few sentences. "I hope you can say goodbye to your father, Josiah. You deserve happiness and you know what you want—go after it. Life is too short to be mired down by things you can't change."

Leah signed the letter with love and slid it into the envelope. She grabbed the telephone book and looked up the address for Josiah's firm. She marked the letter "personal." This correspondence would not rest under a blotter for years. It wasn't closure for her but Leah prayed it would be for him. This was a message she wanted Josiah to read.

She placed the sealed letter next to her purse. She needed to run by the post office to have her mail forwarded. She could mail it then. Josiah would read her letter after she arrived in Atlanta.

And hopefully he would understand that she cared and was sorry for the unintentional hurt she'd caused him. Then she bowed her head and prayed his life, and hers, would be better in the future.

Chapter 16

Josiah left the office around six on Friday evening. Leah should be home by now. He'd come with no plans, thinking they could walk and talk. For two weeks he'd mulled the situation over in his head and had no idea why he thought she would forgive him. He just knew he had to tell her he loved her. He wouldn't blame her if she didn't speak to him.

At her building, he pressed the bell for Leah's unit for the fifth time. Where was she?

A woman walked up and glanced at him as he stepped aside for her to key her entry code.

She looked at him again as if trying to place him. "Oh, hi. You're Leah's friend. I'm sorry but I'm terrible with names."

He remembered Leah introducing them one night when he brought her home. "Josiah Byrd. I wanted to see her but she's not home. Guess I'll wait for a while."

"It'll be a long wait. She moved out today."

Leah had moved? Where had she gone? She loved her condo. "Do you know where she went?"

The woman smiled. "She has a job in Atlanta. She left this afternoon."

Atlanta? A job? Why was she going to Atlanta? She belonged here in Wilmington. With him. "Thanks for the information."

Josiah called the words as he raced to his car. He would go see her parents. Surely they would tell him where to find her. He drove as fast as possible, hating the long uneven lines of traffic that blocked his way. A relieved sigh slipped out when Josiah cleared the worst of it and turned off Market Street into the residential neighborhood where the Wrights lived. As he turned onto their street, he spotted Leah's vehicle parked in her parents' driveway. She hadn't left yet.

Pausing briefly outside his car, Josiah swiped at the moisture beading on his forehead. When almost overcome by the need to run away, he spoke softly to himself. "You can do this. You have to do this now."

Josiah had to tell Leah she made a difference in him and he loved her with all his heart.

He rang the bell and knocked on the Wrights' front door but there was no answer. What was it tonight with people not answering their door? He realized they were probably on the patio enjoying the late August evening. He walked around to the side gate and called "Anyone home?"

"We're here. Come on back."

He hurried into the backyard, his gaze finding Leah as she jumped up from her reclining position on the chaise longue at the sight of him. "Josiah? What are you doing here?"

"Hope I'm not interrupting."

"Not at all," Marty said. "Come sit down. Can we get you something to drink? Leah made a pitcher of lemonade."

"That would be wonderful. Don't get up. I'll help myself."

Josiah pulled a disposable cup from the package and

poured the icy lemonade. He took a sip and it felt good against the dryness of his throat.

Marty Wright smiled and said, "Come have a seat. How have you been?"

"Staying busy. Doing a lot of thinking."

"Did it hurt?" Leah flashed him a cheeky grin.

He smiled back at her. "Surprisingly little."

Ben jumped into the conversation. "What brings you our way?"

"I need to talk to Leah. Can we please talk in private?" His blue gaze pleaded with her to say yes.

She glanced at her parents and back at Josiah. "Sure." She stood. "We can go inside."

In her parents' living room, they sat on opposite ends of the sectional sofa. Lady strolled into the room and jumped up into Leah's lap.

"You're leaving?"

He noted her hesitation. Finally, Leah nodded. "I have a job in Atlanta. I start work on Tuesday."

"What about your work here?"

She frowned. "I can barely support myself."

Panicked, he said, "Don't go. Stay. I'll give you a job."

Her shocked expression told him this was not what she'd expected to hear.

"I need more than a couple weeks of work, Josiah. It's time I stopped allowing my life to control me."

He noticed that she wouldn't look at him. She smoothed a hand over the cat, playing with her as Lady batted at her teasing fingers. "You are in control, Leah. Do you really want to leave your parents and the city where you've spent most of your life?"

"No, but sometimes we don't have a choice."

"You do have a choice. I'm asking you to stay. And not for a short stint organizing my condo. You can work in the office. I don't care if you organize the place or teach organizing classes."

She looked almost hopeful. "You're not being practical."

"I'm trying to tell you I love you and I don't want you to go. You need to stay so we can get to know each other better and you'll marry me. We'll move into Mom's house and raise our babies there."

That got her attention. "Josiah?"

Crestfallen, he asked, "You don't love me?"

"No. I mean, yes, I do." She looked flustered.

"You do?" Hope leaped within him.

"Yes. That's another reason I decided to leave. I didn't want to be in the same city and never see you."

He leaned closer. "You can see me all the time. Every day for the rest of your life. I've missed you, Leah."

"You didn't call." The accusatory words mirrored her pouty expression.

"I've been working on myself. Trying to change who I am."

"I liked who you were."

He smiled. "You'll like the new and improved me more. I've prayed about these feelings and I'm happy to say I've realized the importance of forgiveness. I stepped out of the world of denial I've been living in for years. I can't take the blame for the things I couldn't control and I can't be responsible for Mom's happiness and well-being."

Confused, she said, "But I have this job."

"Plans change. They'll find someone else." Josiah hoped she would agree. He didn't want to live without her.

"Kim's expecting me. She's offered me her spare room. Probably gone to a lot of trouble getting it ready for me."

"She'd understand if you tell her you're in love and can't go."

"Why are you doing this now? I haven't seen you in weeks.

Why would you show up when I've finally gotten my life on track?"

"I was afraid?"

Her skeptical look told him she wasn't buying that. "Afraid of what?"

"That I won't be a good husband and father. That I'll be like my dad and grandfather."

"Sure, you'll be like them. You have their blood running through your veins. But you'll be you. You would be there for your kids. And if you were my husband you'd be there for me, just as I would for you. Marriage is a partnership, Josiah. Both parties have to give far more than they ever hope to get back to have a successful marriage."

"That's why I need you in my life. You don't hold back."

"You aren't a kid, Josiah. You're a grown man who runs a successful business. Why would you have doubts?"

"Because it's not always about being successful. Careers are great but love is better. Knowing the people you love will stand beside you through thick and thin."

"Did you doubt I would be there for you when this thing happened with Cecily?"

"That's just it. I didn't think. I reacted. And I was ashamed."

"Too ashamed to talk?"

Josiah stood and fished in his pocket. He pulled out a round cut diamond engagement ring with smaller diamonds running down each side. "I bought this ring a week ago. It took me that long to convince myself that you wouldn't throw me out. I went to your place tonight, hoping we could make up. When your neighbor said you'd left this afternoon, my first thought was I had to find you. I would have driven to Atlanta just to tell you how I feel."

He dropped to one knee. "Leah, I love you so much. I don't want to rush you. I know we need more time to know each other, but will you please consider marrying me?"

She met his gaze. "When did you realize you loved me?"

Lady turned up her nose and jumped off Leah's lap. Josiah took her hands in his. "I think the feeling snuck up on me from the beginning. I just know that it became important to speak to you. To see you. To spend time with you."

"And then you accused me of being disloyal."

"I'm truly sorry about that. If it makes you any happier, Mom gave me what for when she heard what had happened."

She moved forward into his arms, her hands smoothing his face. "I didn't want that."

"I know. She didn't say anything I didn't need to hear."

"Is she the reason you came here tonight?"

He shook his head in denial. "I know I've been an idiot about this, Leah. I let the most important person in my life slip away because of my fears."

"Let it go, Josiah."

He nodded. "I have. Mom and I agree it's time to move on with our futures. She's happy with Peter. He treats her well and they enjoy each other's company."

"I'm glad. Uncle Peter is a good guy."

"She doesn't know I planned to ask you to marry me. This is between us. So what do you say? Will you stay? Give me a chance to prove how much I love you?"

Josiah sensed her indecision. He prayed she wouldn't walk away from him.

Her head moved slowly from side to side. "I can't. I've accepted this job and I need to do this. I've been so frustrated over the path my life is taking. And I want to finish my thesis."

When he rose and started to walk away, Leah shot up off the sofa and grabbed his arm. "Wait. It's temporary. Two months. I've prayed, seeking God's guidance and feel He's directing my path. I need to do this. For me."

"I can't bear the thought of being away from you for two seconds much less two months."

"We've just spent weeks apart."

"Because I was stupid."

"No." Leah shook her head firmly. "You were confused. I'm not a fan of long-distance relationships but we can communicate while we're apart. There's the telephone, Skype, email. Atlanta is only seven hours away by car and less than that by plane. Please, Josiah. I need to do this."

Everything in Josiah said no. He wanted to drop to his knees and beg but understood that Leah had to follow her heart. He nodded. "We will communicate. And I'll come visit you in Atlanta every chance I get."

Leah flung her arms about his neck and hugged him. "Thank you for understanding."

Josiah held her tight. He couldn't say he understood but he wouldn't stand in the way of her doing what she felt she had to do.

"Anything you want. Our initial meeting may have been unintentional but make no mistake about it, I'm yours and have no intention of giving up on us."

"I won't give up on you either, Josiah. I love you."

He kissed her, savoring the uniqueness of the beautiful young woman he longed to call his wife.

Epilogue

Six months later

"You may kiss your bride."

Josiah folded back her veil and kissed Leah to the applause of their assorted guests.

She touched his cheek and whispered, "I love you."

He winked and shifted his coat slightly so she could see the envelope he had placed over his heart. "I love you."

Josiah treasured her letter to him and carried it over his heart on their wedding day. For him, that letter received after her departure had become a statement of her love, written before he had come to her.

The pastor indicated they should turn to face their families and friends. "And now it is my happy privilege to congratulate and introduce to you Mr. and Mrs. Josiah Byrd."

They paused briefly, Leah taking her bouquet of white roses and calla lilies with green leaves from Kim. Josiah held her hand as they took their first steps down the aisle. They paused by the front pews to kiss their mothers and then hurried toward the open doors, smiling so big with their joy they were surprised their faces didn't crack.

Once outside, Josiah swung her around. "Ready for Paris, Mrs. Byrd?"

"Definitely."

Marty came outside a few minutes later. "The photographers are waiting."

"We'll be right there, Mom."

Josiah shook his head in disbelief. "Still can't believe you want a book of photos cluttering up your life."

She squeezed his arm. "Okay, I finally got what our moms meant by holding on to your memories. Those wedding photos will be treasures I plan to hold on to with all my might. I'll share them with our kids and we'll look at them often to remember this wonderful day."

He kissed her. "We will. Let's go see that photographer."

The time apart had been even worse than the time they'd missed out on because of Josiah's doubts. Leah liked to think their love had grown with their ability to communicate. They'd learned how to say what needed to be said when the opportunity presented itself instead of waiting for later. Josiah had traveled to Atlanta about once a month and Leah had flown home twice with her most recent visit being for Thanksgiving. Her parents had been so disappointed by her practicality when she said she'd be home for Christmas but not Thanksgiving that Leah had bought a ticket. Josiah, Cecily and Uncle Peter had joined them and it had been a wonderful holiday.

When her job had been extended for an additional month, Josiah protested, saying he needed her to come home. She had promised him that she would come soon. Leah's feelings of self-worth had escalated with the praise she'd received from the staff. She'd even progressed with her thesis. Kim had been very helpful in moving the process along.

On her last weekend in Atlanta, Josiah had flown in to join her on the drive back. Leah greeted him with a hug and kiss. It had only been a week since she'd seen him but it seemed more like forever.

"They offered me another extension on my job," she told him that night over dinner.

"What are you going to do?"

She shrugged. "It's good experience for a résumé."

He had learned that the Wright women needed to make their own decisions. "Tell you what. The Children's Christmas Parade is tomorrow. Let's bundle up and go enjoy ourselves."

Leah liked the idea. "And there's an indoor Christmas festival I wanted to see."

"I saw that Macy's has the tree-lighting with performers and fireworks. Okay, we've got a plan to overdose on Christmas. We'll have fun tomorrow and think about the future on Sunday."

They managed two of the three events and went out to dinner Saturday night.

"Can we please talk about the job thing? It's driving me crazy."

"What do you want to do, Leah?"

"I like the work and the people but I miss you and my parents."

Josiah reached into his coat pocket and set the jewelry box on the table. "Is this still in play?"

Her engagement ring. Though she'd never put it on her hand, Leah knew without a doubt that she would wear the ring. "Yes. Today I watched those families and the enjoyment on the kids' faces and I knew that's what I really want out of life."

He reached for her hand. "It's yours. Do you want me to drop down on bended knee and ask you again?"

Leah had read of fabulous engagements and imagined what her own would be like but in truth the look in Josiah's eyes at this very moment said all there was to say. He loved her. And she loved him. "Yes, Josiah. I want to be your wife."

He slipped the ring in place and moved closer in the booth to seal the promise with a kiss.

They called their parents to share the news and the next day he helped her pack her SUV. On Monday, Leah visited the company to refuse the extension and thanked them for giving her the opportunity. Kim agreed that love was the most important factor. And Leah felt at peace as they drove home to Wilmington together. This was the plan for her.

Once they made up their minds to get married, neither wanted to wait the year their mothers claimed it would take to plan a wedding. Marty and Cecily argued there was no way to plan a wedding in three months but Leah and Josiah assured them it could and would be done.

"It's going to be a small wedding," Leah said. "That alone will help with the time frame."

But it wasn't meant to be. Despite the fact that they were only children, there were relatives, friends and clients and before they knew it the guest list numbered two hundred people. Both mothers were excited but Josiah and Leah couldn't say the same.

Because of the size of their party, they opted to hold the reception at a beautiful resort hotel at Wrightsville Beach.

Their mothers insisted they register for gifts and when the items started pouring in, Leah was beside herself. "What are we going to do with all this stuff?"

"Well, we do have access to this huge house. I think the dining room can fit a table to hold all twelve place settings of your favorite china."

"We'll never have that many guests for dinner."

"We already have six people. You could exchange it for something else you need. Or wait and see what the future holds."

"It's not going to hold ten children," she said dryly.

He chuckled. "No one said you have to have them all. We could always adopt or foster kids."

"Let's not get carried away just yet. We'll be new to this parenting business and don't want to get in over our heads before we even get started."

The mothers insisted on going with Leah when she shopped for her dress. When they pleaded with her to at least try on a princess gown, Leah did as requested. They immediately saw she wasn't going to be happy in so much dress. She stuck to her guns and chose a slim line style fitted gown of tulle overlay veiling a delicate lace sheath with a V-neckline and cap sleeves. Earlier, both women had gasped when she stepped out in the gown with her hair pulled up in loose curls and her fingertip veil.

Marty took her hands and held out her arms as she took in the beauty before her. "You chose the perfect dress."

"Thanks, Mom. They won't even see me with two class acts like you and Cecily coming out first."

Marty wore a beautifully fitted long sage green V-neck gown, while Cecily had opted for an A-line V-neck floor length taffeta dress with lace beading. The pale pink color suited her lightly tanned skin.

Like Leah's father, Peter had dressed in a black tuxedo, to escort his new fiancée down the aisle. No one had been surprised when he popped the question a couple of weeks before. Cecily had agreed immediately. Peter owned a home at Wrightsville Beach and after the wedding they would live there when they weren't traveling.

In fact, Cecily and Marty got on so well that they planned

to take a trip together with their husbands in the future. They had done all kinds of research to decide where they wanted to go first.

Her father had teased them about putting the clinic out of business by taking both dentists away. Peter said he'd been thinking of retiring and suggested they find another partner to run their business in their absence.

Today, Kim wore the orchid bridesmaid dress. Susan wanted to be there but her advancing pregnancy kept her off her feet. Kim talked about how much she was going to miss having Leah at her apartment. Josiah promised to send pictures.

Thoughts of the problems caused by that first letter still caused Leah regrets but when she considered how the unintentional act had changed so many lives, she knew a power greater than any of them had been in control.

"Leah, you ready for those pictures?"

She winked at Josiah. "Yes, my love. Let's make some wonderful memories of our own."

* * * * *

REQUEST YOUR FREE BOOKS!

2 FREE CHRISTIAN NOVELS
PLUS 2
FREE
MYSTERY GIFTS

HEARTSONG

PRESENTS

LARGER-PRINT BOOKS!

GET 2 FREE
LARGER-PRINT NOVELS
PLUS 2 FREE
MYSTERY GIFTS

Love Inspired®

Larger-print novels are now available...

LILPDIR13R

When helicopter pilot Creed Carter finds an abandoned baby
on a church altar, he must convince foster parent
Haley Blanchard that she'll make a good mom—and a
good match.

Baby in His Arms

by ## Linda Goodnight

Former gunslinger Hunter Mitchell wants to start his life over
with his newly discovered nine-year-old daughter–and his best
chance at providing his daughter a stable home is a marriage of
convenience to her beautiful and fiercely protective teacher.

Charity
HOUSE

The Outlaw's Redemption

by

RENEE RYAN

Available July 2013.

www.LoveInspiredBooks.com

LIH2971

Love Inspired
SUSPENSE
RIVETING INSPIRATIONAL ROMANCE

Someone is after Tessa Camry—but only she knows why. Now she
must depend on bodyguard Seth Sinclair to keep her safe from
her past...and give her a reason to look forward to the future.

HEROES
for HIRE

DEFENDER
FOR HIRE
by
SHIRLEE MCCOY

Available July 2013 wherever books are sold.

LIS4544

HARLEQUIN®

A *Romance* FOR EVERY MOOD™

Stay up-to-date on all your
romance-reading news with the
Harlequin Shopping Guide,
featuring bestselling authors, exciting new
miniseries, books to watch and more!

The newest issue will be delivered right to you
with our compliments! There are 4 each year.

Signing up is easy.

EMAIL

ShoppingGuide@Harlequin.ca

WRITE TO US

HARLEQUIN BOOKS
Attention: Customer Service Department
P.O. Box 9057, Buffalo, NY 14269-9057

OR PHONE

1-800-873-8635 in the United States
1-888-343-9777 in Canada

Please allow 4-6 weeks for delivery of the first issue by mail.

Ouvrage reproduit
par procédé photomécanique.
Impression Bussière
à Saint-Amand (Cher), le 2 janvier 2006.
Dépôt légal : janvier 2006.
1er dépôt légal : octobre 2000.
Numéro d'imprimeur : 054602/1.
ISBN 2-07-041611-9./Imprimé en France.